AF416400

Magnolia Jane

Magnolia Jane

HOLLY JO FLORA

Magnolia Jane

Copyright © 2026 by Holly Jo Flora

ISBN 979-8-9911567-8-3

All rights reserved.

No part of this publication may be reproduced, distributed, or transmitted in any form or by any means, including photocopying, recording, or other electronic or mechanical methods, without the prior written permission of the author. For permission requests, contact Holly Jo Flora.

The story, all names, characters, and incidents portrayed in this book are fictitious. No identification with actual persons (living or deceased), places, buildings, and products is intended or should be inferred.

Cover Art by Heather at Smittenware

Cover Design by Julie May and Holly Jo Flora

Formatting by Holly Jo Flora

Author Photo by Taylor Haynie

1   2   3   4   5   6   7   8   9   10

To Alex

Chapter 1

Maggie's office phone rang.

"Hello?"

"May I please speak with Magnolia Jane Shaw?"

"This is she," Maggie said as she snatched the papers waiting in her copier. She had only two minutes until the company meeting started.

"This is Oliver Moore. I'm an attorney at Moore and Turner Law Firm in Newton County, Arkansas. Ms. Shaw, I regret to inform you that your grandmother, Edith Patton, passed away last week."

"Oh, ummm—I believe you have the wrong person. Both of my grandmothers died years ago." Maggie grabbed her purse and a stack of folders as she stood.

"There's no mistake, ma'am. Your mother was Rebekah Hannah Shaw, and Edith Patton was your mother's mother.

I'm aware that your mother told you her parents passed away before you were born, but that isn't true."

Maggie slowly sat back down in her desk chair.

Oliver continued, "I realize this news comes as a surprise."

"Are you sure? My mom . . . Mom *told* me her parents both died while she was pregnant with me."

"Yes, I'm sure. I met with Mrs. Edith a couple of years ago when she had me draw up her will. She explained to me that her granddaughter—you, Ms. Shaw—had been told that she was dead."

"Wh-why? Why was I . . . lied to?"

"Mrs. Edith didn't go into the details with me, ma'am. What she *did* do, however, was leave an inheritance and an envelope for you."

Maggie sat there, absorbing what she'd just heard. She shook her head quickly, as if breaking a trance.

"I'm sorry." She swallowed. "This all—this is such a shock."

"It must be. I'm sorry to surprise you with all this news. Once you've had time to process it, could we please schedule a meeting?"

"Yes, yes, of course. You said you were from Newton County?"

"Yes, ma'am. Your grandmother lived in Jasper. I'd like for us to meet there, if that's possible."

"Okay, let me see if I can get off work tomorrow. Would that be too soon? I mean, do you have an opening then?"

"I could meet you any time after twelve."

"Okay." Maggie looked at the caller ID on her office phone. "Can I call you back at this number to let you know if I'm able to meet?"

"Yes, ma'am, that would be fine. This is my work cell."

"Okay, thank you, Mr. Moore," Maggie replied, grabbing a pen and writing down the number on her notepad. "I'll get back to you soon."

"Sounds good. Goodbye, Ms. Shaw."

"Bye."

Maggie hung up and froze, her hand resting on her office phone. She jumped when her cell rang.

"Hello?"

"Maggie, where are you?" Hadley whispered. "Your presentation's first."

Maggie grabbed her purse and papers. "I'm on my way!"

"An inheritance?" Hadley asked as she set her fork down on her plate.

"That's what he said," Maggie answered.

Hadley was Maggie's closest friend. They'd shared an office for a year after both being hired at Designly Inc. After the company meeting, Maggie and Hadley had walked down the street to their favorite deli for lunch.

"Whoa," said Hadley. "I mean—first off, I'm really sorry about your grandma passing."

"Thank you, but I feel more shocked than sad. I didn't even know she'd been alive until an hour ago, and I feel more confused than shocked. Why did my mom lie to me about her parents? And why did we have nothing to do with them?"

Hadley slowly shook her head and shrugged her shoulders as she chewed a bite of pasta salad.

"And Mom and Dad are gone, so I have no one to ask."

Maggie's parents died four years ago when she was twenty-two. They were in a head-on collision with a drunk driver. Her dad, mom, and the other driver were all killed instantly.

"What about your grandpa?" Hadley asked, opening her

bag of chips. "Think he'd remember?"

"I don't know. He has good days and bad days," Maggie said, taking a bite of her club sandwich.

Maggie's grandfather—her dad's father—was her only living relative. He had Alzheimer's and lived in a memory care facility. Typically, Maggie visited him every Tuesday evening and Saturday morning.

"I'll go see him today when I get off work," said Maggie. "He may have never even met my mom's parents, but who knows?"

"So, you're going to Jasper tomorrow?"

"Yeah, that's another reason I need to go see Grandpa today, because I won't be able to go tomorrow, like I usually do. I talked with Mrs. Anderson after the meeting, and she said I could take tomorrow and Wednesday off if I needed to."

"That's good. Will you call me tomorrow and let me know what your grandma left you? And what her letter says?"

"Of course."

"I'm not trying to make light of anything," said Hadley. "But what if she left you a five-carat diamond ring? Or a million dollars?"

Maggie smiled. "I think the chances of that are super small, but I'd be lying if I said those kinds of thoughts didn't cross my mind during the meeting." She set her remaining sandwich on her plate. "But you know, it all makes me feel . . . I don't know, guilty? Maybe that's the word."

"Why?"

"Just to accept a big gift from someone I never knew, never talked to, never visited."

"Well, your mom must have had a good reason to keep you away." Hadley's eyes grew wide. "Maybe your grandma was a convicted murderer."

"Surely not."

"What if the envelope she left you is a confession disclosing where all the people she killed are buried?"

"Hadley! Stop it. You're gonna creep me out."

"Sorry. I've been watching too many crime shows." Hadley took a sip of her water. "What if she left you her eleven cats? Or a pet snake?"

"Then I'll be swinging by the animal shelter on my way home."

"How long of a drive is it to Jasper?"

"Around three hours. It's crazy . . . isn't it? My grandma lived only three hours away, and I had no idea." Maggie checked the time on her phone. "We'd better get back to work."

Maggie walked up to the front desk at Havenwood Memory Care.

"Maggie Shaw here to see Liam Shaw."

"Yes, ma'am," said the receptionist. As she wrote Maggie's name on a visitor sticker, a large-framed nurse joined them at the counter.

"Hello, hello, Ms. Maggie!" the jolly older woman said. "You're here a day early, aren't you?"

"Hey, Mrs. Patricia," Maggie answered with a smile. "Yes, ma'am. I can't make it tomorrow. How's he doing today?"

"Oh, now, we're havin' a pretty good day. He had no troubles gettin' dressed this mornin', ate up all of his breakfast and lunch, and he's been hummin'—been a good day so far."

After Maggie put her sticker on her shirt, she and Patricia walked down the hall to her grandpa's room. His door was open.

"Mr. Shaw?" Patricia said as she tapped on the door.

"You got company! Maggie has come by to see you."

"Hi!" said Maggie with a smile.

"You need anything, you just push the button or come get me," Patricia whispered.

"Yes, ma'am. Thank you," Maggie quietly replied.

Maggie walked into the room. Her grandpa was sitting in his chair, looking out the window. A tree with purple blossoms grew outside his room, and he frequently sat and watched it sway in the breeze. Maggie sat on a stool near his chair.

"Hello. I'm glad to see you." That was always what she said when she visited. She'd learned not to call him Grandpa or to ask him if he knew who she was.

He smiled back at her. "Well, hello there. How are you?" His eyes were happy today.

"I'm good," Maggie answered. "How are you?"

"I'm good, too. Thank you for asking."

Maggie glanced out the window. "That tree outside sure is pretty, isn't it?"

"Oh, yes. Very pretty. You know, I used to have a tree exactly like that one in my backyard."

He remembered.

"You always had such a well-kept yard," said Maggie.

"I did." He nodded. "I worked really hard to keep it looking good."

"Yes, you did." Maggie set her purse on the table beside her. "I had an interesting phone call today. It was about Edith Patton."

"Edith Patton," her grandpa repeated.

Maggie waited.

He looked into her eyes and raised his eyebrows. "Are you Edith Patton?"

Maggie exhaled the breath she'd been holding. "No, I'm not. My name is Maggie."

"Oh, nice to meet you, Maggie."

She forced a smile. "It's nice to meet you too."

"Peanut! Peanut?" a woman frantically yelled from Liam's doorway.

Maggie and her grandpa jumped in their seats.

"Have y'all seen my dog?" she shouted at them.

The woman was Mrs. Winkle, a patient in the room across the hall. At almost every one of Maggie's visits, Mrs. Winkle would burst into her grandpa's room, loudly searching for her dog. Maggie had learned from Patricia that Peanut had died the year before, right before Mrs. Winkle was admitted to the facility.

"I can't find him anywhere!" Mrs. Winkle said, on the verge of tears.

"I haven't seen him, Mrs. Winkle. I'm so sorry," said Maggie. "Let me go get the nurse. I'm sure she'll be able to help you."

Maggie left to find Patricia with Mrs. Winkle following her down the hall.

When she returned, she found her grandpa still sitting in his chair, but his countenance had changed completely. He was wringing his hands, staring at the floor, and scowling. He kept muttering something.

Maggie slowly knelt down beside him.

"That Edith Patton. She hurt our Rebekah," he said softly to himself. "She and Rodney hurt our Rebekah so badly."

"They hurt Mom?" Maggie asked.

His eyes slowly turned to her and softened.

She put her hand on his knee. "Did they hurt Rebekah?"

He smiled. "Is your name Rebekah?"

Maggie let out a small sigh and calmly answered, "No, my name is Maggie."

Chapter 2

Maggie pulled into the driveway of a quaint brick house. The location surprised her. This was the address Mr. Moore had given her, but she'd assumed they'd meet at a business or a coffee shop. She noticed a beige Toyota Camry in the carport and a gray SUV parked on the grass. As she parked, a middle-aged man wearing khakis and a button-up shirt got out of the SUV. He held a manila envelope in one hand.

"Ms. Magnolia?" he asked as she closed her door.

"Yes, but you can just call me Maggie."

He took off his sunglasses and extended his hand. "Maggie, I'm Oliver Moore."

"Nice to meet you," she replied, shaking his hand.

"Good to meet you, and thank you for coming all this way." Oliver took a set of keys from his pocket. "I have some papers here for you to sign, and then I'll be able to give you what Mrs. Edith left you." He put his sunglasses in his pocket and pulled out a pen. "Would it be okay if we used the back of your car as a makeshift desk?"

"Sure, that'll be fine."

Maggie followed him to the back of her car. Oliver took some papers from the envelope and placed them on top of her trunk. He handed her his pen and showed her where to sign.

"All right, then. As Mrs. Edith's sole heir, these now belong to you." Oliver handed Maggie the manila envelope and the set of keys.

As Maggie took the keys, she looked up at him in confusion.

"The envelope has a personal item of Mrs. Edith's, and the keys are for the house and the car."

"She . . . she left me her *house*?"

"Yes, she did. That's why I thought meeting here would be better than us meeting at my office."

Maggie slowly turned to look again at the house. It was a two-story brick with a small front porch. Excluding the carport, the house was symmetrical. There were four windows on the front—two on the second floor and two on the first, with the front door in between. The windows had dark-brown stained shutters, and the two first-floor windows had flower boxes overflowing with lantanas. The front door was stained the same dark brown as the shutters. The front porch steps were flanked by flower beds filled with pentas and angelonias in full bloom. The house had a bit of a cottage vibe.

"These types of inheritances can be a bit overwhelming. It's not as cut-and-dry as being left with other physical assets, like jewelry or a painting. Hopefully, this will help." Oliver handed Maggie some papers held together with a paper clip. "It's information on what needs to be done when inheriting a home and/or vehicle."

Maggie stared at the top sheet. She was absolutely overwhelmed. Five minutes ago, she owned a car and rented an apartment. Now she had two cars, an apartment, a yard, and a house—undoubtedly filled with her grandmother's belongings. Unbeknownst to Oliver, Maggie knew all too well the work, time, and stress that had just been dumped on her. She'd been through all of this before.

Maggie's parents had also left everything to her when they passed. Which was, of course, a blessing but also a mountain of responsibility and decisions. She tried living there alone for almost a year after her parents died, but she couldn't do it. The memories and the silence in the house were too much, especially at Christmastime. After months of agonizing debate, Maggie sold her childhood home.

"If you'd like to go inside," Oliver said, interrupting her thoughts, "I can walk through the house with you, or I understand if you'd rather be alone."

"I . . . ummm . . . I may, uhhh . . . I may just sit on the porch for a bit and try to get my head around all of this."

Oliver nodded. "That's a good idea. Well, you have my number," he said, putting on his sunglasses. "Please don't hesitate to call me if you have any questions."

"Thank you."

Oliver smiled and nodded again before turning to walk to his vehicle.

"Oh, wait!" Maggie called. As Oliver turned back to her, she ran over to him. "I do have a question. It's one I've meant to ask since we spoke yesterday, but things have happened so fast, I just keep forgetting to ask. How did my grandmother die?"

"She had a heart attack. From what I was told, it was a massive one. She died instantly."

Maggie's eyes darted toward the house and then back to Oliver. "Did she die in the . . . inside the house?"

"No, she was in the backyard working in her garden when it happened."

"Oh dear, was she there a long time before someone

found her?"

"No, her neighbor," Oliver motioned toward the house to their right, "found her not long after it happened. I believe they were close friends and spent a lot of time together."

Maggie stared at the neighbor's house while she thought. "So . . . so I guess my grandma's funeral already happened?"

"Yes, she had a service at her church last Friday and was buried next to your grandfather. Your grandmother specified in her wishes that she didn't want you to know about your inheritance or her passing until *after* she was buried."

Maggie quickly looked back at Oliver, her eyes showing her confusion.

"Your grandmother had her reasons. I don't know or understand all of it, but I think that will give you some answers," Oliver said, motioning to the envelope still in her hand.

After saying goodbye again, Maggie watched Oliver back out and drive away. She looked down at the manila envelope in her hand. She opened it, reached inside, and pulled out a journal.

"Okay, I need to sit," Maggie said to herself, walking to her car.

She opened the passenger door, took out her purse, and set the empty envelope on the car seat. After putting her grandmother's house and car keys into her purse, she grabbed her phone from the cupholder. Maggie locked the car as she climbed the three porch steps. There were two wooden rockers, one on each side of the front door. Sitting down in the one on the left, she placed her purse beside her feet.

Maggie looked down at the green journal in her hands. She inhaled deeply, then exhaled, before opening the cover to the first page. There were only two words written in cursive—

To Magnolia

Chapter 3

Maggie quickly thumbed through the journal's pages. Almost every page was filled with writing. This was going to take far longer than one afternoon of reading on the porch. Her thoughts were interrupted when her phone rang from her purse. She looked at the screen—it was Hadley.

"Hey."

"Well? What did she leave you? I couldn't wait any longer to find out!"

"She left me a journal filled with writing, her car, and her house."

Silence.

"She left you her house?" Hadley finally asked.

"Yep."

"Oh, Maggie. I'm so sorry." Hadley remembered the turmoil Maggie endured when handling her parents' house, vehicles, and belongings—all while grieving.

"It is what it is. Surely this will be much easier than it was with Mom and Dad's. I didn't know my grandmother, so I don't feel tied to any of her things or this house."

"So, you're gonna sell it all?"

"Yeah, I mean, I don't live or work around here. I'll probably line up an estate sale, depending on how much stuff is inside the house, and then I'll have it listed."

"What about the car?"

"Oh, I'll definitely be selling the car. It's old and beige."

"So where are you now?"

"I'm sitting on the porch of her—or, I guess I should say, *my*—house."

"You haven't gone inside yet?"

As Hadley asked, Maggie saw movement out of the corner of her eye. She looked over to see someone watching her from behind the neighbor's curtains. The curtain quickly closed.

"Not yet," said Maggie. "I sat down to read a little of the journal first, but I think the neighbor is watching me." She grabbed her purse and stood. "Honestly, I think I just want to go home now." Maggie hurried down the porch steps toward her car.

"Without checking inside first?"

"Yes, I—I don't know. I don't feel ready to go inside yet, for some reason."

"Maybe you're afraid of what you'll see. Like, what if she was a hoarder, and you can't even walk into the rooms?"

"Hadley, that does not help."

"Sorry."

Maggie started her car. "I guess I wanted to *meet* my grandmother a little by reading what she'd written me before I went inside. But with the neighbor watching me, I feel like I'm in a fishbowl." She backed out of the driveway and got on the road. "I'll read the journal when I get home."

"Will you be at work tomorrow?"

"Mrs. Anderson said I could take tomorrow off, too, so I think I'll stay home and read this journal. I'll be back at work on Thursday."

"What about your grandma's house?"

"I'll come back on Saturday. Hopefully, I'll have a game plan by then."

Maggie opened the door to her apartment. She'd stopped on her way home and picked up a pizza for dinner. While holding the pizza box in one hand, she set her purse, keys, and phone on the foyer table before closing and locking the door. She picked up her phone, took the journal from her purse, and headed to her bedroom, setting the pizza box on the counter as she passed through the kitchen. Once in her room, she set her phone and the journal on her nightstand and changed into pajamas.

Maggie picked up the frame from her nightstand and stared at the photo it displayed—her favorite picture of her parents. She'd taken the photo years ago when her family had visited Biltmore in North Carolina. Her mom and dad were standing on the back porch—if you can call it a porch—of the Biltmore House. The landscape behind them was lush and green, with a panoramic view of endless trees and the Blue Ridge Mountains. Her parents looked so happy, so content. Her mom's head was leaning against her dad's shoulder.

Maggie stared at her mom's face.

"Why so many secrets?" she whispered.

Maggie gently returned the frame to the nightstand and went to the kitchen. She grabbed a drink and the pizza box and set them on the coffee table in the living room. After plopping onto the couch, she opened the box, bowed her head, closed her eyes, and said, "Thank you, Lord, for this food." Her dad or mom had said those six words every time before they'd eaten as a family. Ever since they died, Maggie said the same prayer before eating.

She turned on the TV and took a bite of her pizza. While eating, she kept clicking through the channels, never settling on any show or movie. Her brain wasn't paying attention to the TV. She was mentally going through the happenings of the day. She felt torn. She wanted to dive into the journal and hopefully find answers, but at the same time, the thought of doing so felt overwhelming and exhausting.

She decided to put away the leftover pizza, email her boss, get ready for bed, and then start reading the journal. She'd probably be up all night because her brain was too awake to sleep.

Maggie reached for the journal. Sliding down into the blankets on her bed, she lay back and got comfortable.

"Okay, here we go," she said to herself.

Opening the book, she read the words again:

To Magnolia

She turned the page.

November 1, 2024

Magnolia,

I've been sitting here for at least half an hour, trying to figure out how to start this. I guess I should introduce myself. My name is Edith Shirley Patton, and I'm your grandmother. I know we've never met before, and I know your mother told you that her father and I passed away years ago. I want to explain all of that to you, or I guess, explain what I now understand . . . what I now know. I know that I was wrong, very wrong to your mother. I'd give anything to go back and do things—do everything differently. But I can't.

I don't want to disrupt your life, and I hope I'm not. You're just my only living relative now. Yes, I know about the accident. I'm so sorry about Rebekah and Jacob. My heart broke when I found out. They were both so young.

I almost came to their funerals, but Rebekah would not have wanted that. She told me that she never wanted you to meet her father or me. I wanted to respect her wishes; that's the least I could do for her after what happened. So, I continued to stay away. I also knew you were going through so much when they died. I feared that suddenly showing up after you'd been told I was dead would add too much drama to an already unbelievably difficult time for you. I hope I made the right decision.

Chapter 4

I guess I should explain my upbringing.

I was born in 1964. I came from a religious family. My father, mother, sisters, and I were active in our church. We were there any time the doors were open.

My dad was a stern man. He was very much in charge of our family. He made all the decisions and didn't allow any backtalk. His word was law. My mother was a meek woman. I don't ever remember her arguing with my father. My sisters and I were raised to never question or disobey him.

When I was eighteen, Rodney Patton came to our house. He worked with my father. I didn't know at the time, but apparently my father and Rodney had decided that I was a good match for him. I remember being called into the family room, and my father introducing us. He said, "Rodney has my blessing to date you." I was never asked, which didn't bother me back then. I was so used to my father making decisions for me that this seemed normal. And I trusted my father. I was excited because, as my mother put it, "He had found the man God had for me."

Seven months later, Rodney and I were married. He was like my father in some ways, but there was a cruelness about him that was not like my father. Rodney would sometimes have to "discipline me." He'd hit me with his belt or smack me across my face. Then he'd tell me that I made him do those things. I'd been taught that God wants women to obey their husbands, and that divorce is a sin, so I accepted my life.

Eleven months after we were married, I had Rebekah. It was an extremely difficult delivery. Rodney insisted that it be a home birth and would not allow me to go to the hospital. He said women had been doing this for thousands of years and that we weren't going to pay a pointless hospital bill. He didn't stay during the delivery. He said I was being too loud and dramatic. A lady from our church, who worked as a midwife, delivered Rebekah. Immediately after giving birth, I lost consciousness from losing too much blood. The midwife had to call an ambulance. After being rushed to the hospital, I received a blood transfusion and medicine to control the hemorrhage. They kept me overnight so I could be monitored. Rodney made me pay for all of that . . . and not with money.

Becoming a mother showed me that I really was a lot like my mother. I didn't argue or push issues; I obeyed. Rebekah was completely different. She had this strong will—even as a toddler—that tested everything and everyone. Rodney would not allow that. He "disciplined" her often. Honestly, at that time, I found myself upset with Rebekah. I'm embarrassed and ashamed to write that, but it's the truth. I blamed her for constantly setting him off. She was such a willful child.

We never had more children, which was very upsetting to Rodney. He wanted a son and was disappointed in me for not being able to give him one. I don't know if some damage had been done during Rebekah's delivery or if God didn't want us to have more children.

In the early nineties—I can't remember the exact date—Rodney wanted us to attend a seminar by a non-denominational organization he'd heard about at work. We did, and that changed everything. The seminar's main speaker was the organization's founder, and Rodney agreed with everything he said.

We soon joined the organization. Over the next year, Rodney stopped allowing me to wear makeup. Rebekah and I had to wear long dresses or skirts at all times and grow our hair long. We pulled Rebekah out of school because "I needed to homeschool her." We got rid of our television and radio. Only music played on the piano was permitted, and that could only be hymns. We could never dance or go to the movies.

The organization taught that in order for God to bless your family, the husband/father had to be the leader and head of the home in all ways. The wife and children were under him and must always be submissive. We were also taught to have as many children as possible because this was pleasing to God. The other families in the organization would have ten or more children. Our small family size always embarrassed Rodney. He told me many times that I failed him as a wife in this area.

It matters to me that you know this: Rebekah and I did have many good times together. I taught her how to cook, sew, can vegetables, and play the piano. Those truly are some of my favorite memories, when it was just the two of us, and we didn't have to walk on eggshells.

We had only one vehicle, so Rebekah and I usually stayed at home. She or I rarely went anywhere. Our typical outings were just once a week to the grocery store, and we, of course, went to church.

When Rebekah was sixteen, our pastor's wife let us know she would be teaching free calligraphy classes at the library. She had two slots still available and wanted to know if Rebekah and Sarah, Rebekah's friend from church, would like to attend. Typically, Rodney would never have allowed her or me to do anything fun like that . . . he enjoyed telling us no to things we were excited about or wanted to do. He liked the control.

I also figured he'd say no because how would Rebekah get there? He had the car during the day. Thankfully, Sarah's mom offered to pick Rebekah up and take the girls to the classes. To our shock, Rodney gave her permission to go. I guess it shouldn't have shocked us; it was our pastor's wife asking for the girls to come to her class. Rodney wanted to get on good terms with our pastor so he would be asked to fill the pulpit when our pastor was out of town or sick.

Rodney, of course, had rules for Rebekah. He always did. He told her she was not allowed to view any of the books in the library because "most of them were ungodly trash."

Rebekah loved the classes. They met every Tuesday and made cards and scripture wall art. They donated most of their creations to the homebound of our church, but I still have one of her pieces hanging in my house. I treasure it.

I want Mom's calligraphy piece, Maggie thought.

Setting the journal down, she grabbed her phone and typed herself a note: **Get Mom's wall art.**

She picked up the journal and resumed reading.

The class met for eight weeks. I thought Rebekah enjoyed it because she was finally getting out of the house, learning something new, and spending time with her friend.

I had no idea what was really going on.

Chapter 5

During the first four weeks, Sarah's mom drove the girls to the calligraphy class, but halfway through the eight weeks, Sarah got her driver's license. After that, Sarah would pick up Rebekah. The class was during the summer, so the girls didn't have school during those weeks.

When the class at the library was over, around mid-July, Rebekah asked me every few days if she could go over to Sarah's house. I was happy that she and Sarah had become closer friends. I knew Rodney would say no, so I didn't ask him. Sarah would come and pick her up and then bring her back again before Rodney got home from work. I saw no harm in it. Sarah's family wasn't as "dedicated and faithful as we were"—that's how Rodney described them—I guess because Sarah and her sisters wore a little makeup. But I thought Rebekah would be safe at their house because Sarah had no brothers, and her dad was at work when Rebekah would be there.

The next part I share will probably feel a bit abrupt, and like it came out of nowhere, but that's exactly how it felt for me when it happened. Looking back, I guess there were probably some clues, but I honestly didn't see any. What happened wasn't even within my mental realm of possibilities.

On January 7, 2000—I'll never forget that day— Rodney and I found out that Rebekah was pregnant. She was seventeen years old. I know her pregnancy age doesn't surprise you at all because, at some point, you undoubtedly put it together that your mother was only seventeen years older than you. But Rodney and I were shocked.

When she told us, or actually, when she told me,

she was three months along. I can still see that moment in my mind. Rodney had left for work. Rebekah and I were cleaning up the kitchen after breakfast. She was unusually quiet that morning. I handed her the bowl I'd just washed for her to dry, and as she took it, she said, "Mom, I need to talk to you." I could see in her eyes that this was something serious.

We sat down at the table, and she said, "I'm pregnant."

My first reaction was to chuckle and tell her that she wasn't. I'd never had "the talk" with her, so I didn't think she even knew about all of that yet, and when on earth could "that" have ever happened? She was never around any boys!

Then she told me everything. I remember listening and feeling numb. It was the weirdest, most surreal feeling.

She met Jacob—your father—at the calligraphy class. Apparently, his grandmother had wanted to attend the class, but she was in a wheelchair and unable to get there. Her grandson was home from college for the summer, so she asked him to take her to the lessons. She surprised Jacob by signing not only herself up for the class, but him too. Apparently, she wanted them to do it together as a bonding-type activity. He didn't want to take calligraphy lessons with a bunch of middle-aged to elderly women, but he did it for his grandmother.

At the first class, Rebekah and Sarah sat at a table with Jacob and his grandmother. That's where they met. After that, they always sat together during each class. At the last lesson, Jacob asked Rebekah if he could see her more. She and Sarah concocted a plan, and as you've probably already put together, every time Sarah picked up Rebekah, she didn't take her to her house; she took her to meet up with Jacob.

When she told me that part, that's when the anger set in. I was furious. She lied to me. She used me. She was unmarried and pregnant, and I knew Rodney would explode on us.

I wish I'd sat there with her and listened more. I wish I had hugged her. She was crying. But instead, I got up and grabbed the phone off the wall. She begged me to please not call her dad yet, but that's exactly what I did. I don't know if I thought that telling him and showing him how angry I was at her might prevent him from coming after me too, or . . . I don't know.

Rodney was home in fifteen minutes. He was terrifying. He stormed in, walked right up to her, and slapped her so hard across her face that it made her nose bleed. He grabbed her jacket from the wall hook, then her arm. He kept shouting that she disgraced him, she humiliated him, she was no longer his daughter, she was dead to us, she was never allowed to set foot back in his house, she'd chosen to follow the devil, and so on. He threw her and her jacket out onto the porch before he slammed and locked the door.

I should have gone after her, but I couldn't have even if I'd tried. Rodney beat me like he never had before because, according to him, this was my fault too.

I didn't know where Rebekah had gone. That night, while Rodney was in the bathroom, I looked out the window—as much as I could through my swollen eyes—onto the porch, and she was gone.

The next morning, while Rodney ate his breakfast, he told me that every photo of Rebekah in our home better be gone when he got home that day, or I'd get it again. He said she was never allowed back into his house, and that from that day on, our daughter was dead.

I cried the entire day. My heart and body ached. I packed up all the picture frames and put them in the attic. I prayed that Rodney wouldn't burn them or throw them away. I called Sarah's house, but she refused to speak to me.

It wasn't until a few months later that I finally found out where and how Rebekah was.

Chapter 6

Maggie tossed the journal onto her bed, near her feet. Hot tears poured down her face. She reached into her nightstand drawer and pulled out a small box of tissues, using one to wipe her eyes and nose.

She'd known for a long time that her mom was seventeen and her dad was nineteen when they'd had her, but she had no idea of the circumstances.

Maggie sat on the edge of her bed and cried.

She had asked a few times about her mom's parents and her childhood, but her mom always responded with something like, "Sweetie, I don't want to talk about that," or "Maggie, that's too painful for Mom to talk about." Maggie had thought it was too difficult for her mom to discuss her past because she missed her parents so much. Now she understood why. Her mom had a monster for a father, and she'd been abandoned by her parents as a pregnant teenager.

She grabbed the journal and went into the next room, where her desk, bookshelves, and treadmill were. Even though it was almost two in the morning, she hopped on her treadmill and started walking slowly. She had too much adrenaline to lie in her bed and read.

She opened the journal again.

At the end of June, Sarah's mom called one morning and let me know that Rebekah had delivered her baby—a girl—the week before. Rebekah had called Sarah and filled her in on everything. I asked where and how Rebekah and the baby were. She told me that since the day Rebekah had been thrown out of our house, she'd been living with Jacob's family, and that both she and you were doing well. I asked more questions—like what your name was—but she stopped me and said that she didn't feel comfortable getting any more involved. She just wanted to let me know that my daughter was safe and healthy.

I was thankful, of course, but also upset. I missed Rebekah. I wanted to meet you, but I couldn't. Rodney would never have allowed it. I never told him about the phone call. He'd have gotten angry and probably violent. To him, Rebekah was dead. But she wasn't to me. She never was.

Now I'll jump ahead to early 2011. Rodney was diagnosed with cancer. It was terrible. I took care of him the best I could. He only lived for five months after his diagnosis.

His death brought on so many emotions. The strongest one was honestly relief. The next was fear. I'd never had a job before and needed to find a way to make an income. I had very few skills and no experience. A lady at church suggested that I start teaching piano lessons, and that's what I did. I also expanded my gardens so I could sell vegetables, canned goods, and flowers at our town's farmers' markets.

Rodney's death gave me freedom. I was free to take all the photos of Rebekah out of the attic and hang them back up! I was free to drive and go anywhere I wanted. I was free to make what I wanted to eat for dinner and to wear what I wanted. Rodney's passing also brought me hope. I hoped I'd finally be able to reconnect with Rebekah and meet you.

I had no idea where to start because I didn't know Jacob's last name, if he and Rebekah had gotten married, or if they were still together. I didn't even know your first name.

A few months after Rodney's death, I drove to Janet's house—Janet was Sarah's mother. I begged her to please give me any information she had on Rebekah. Since Rodney was no longer in the picture, she told me that Rebekah and Jacob had gotten married a few months after you were born. Their last name was Shaw, and your name was Magnolia. She didn't know where you all lived, but she remembered that your family had moved away from Newton County when Jacob graduated from college because he'd gotten a job in a big city.

I didn't have a computer at my house, so I went to the library. I thought finding Rebekah and you would take forever, but the librarian helped me look you all up in a matter of minutes! You were living just outside of Tulsa, Oklahoma. The librarian wrote down your address and phone number for me. I was shocked at how easy it was to find you all!

I went home and wrote Rebekah a letter. I let her know about her father's passing and asked how she and you were. I wanted to ask her if I could please visit and meet you, but I was afraid that might be too much too soon. I thought I'd wait until I received a letter back before asking, but I never got one.

After three weeks of no reply, I wrote her another letter. No reply. Then another letter. This went on and on for months. I finally worked up the nerve to call. I thought perhaps the address was wrong, and maybe Rebekah wasn't receiving any of my letters. So, I called.

I know you won't remember this, Magnolia, but you and I talked on the phone for a few seconds. I called, and you answered. You had the sweetest voice. I asked if I could please speak to Rebekah. You said, "Yes, ma'am," and I heard you call out, "Mom!" Then you told me, "She's on her way." After a moment, Rebekah said, "Hello?" I said, "Rebekah? It's Mom." I heard a gasp.

And then she hung up.

I cried all night.

The next week, I received a letter from Rebekah.

Magnolia, I've tucked your mother's letter to me between the next two pages of this journal. I want you to read it. I hope it helps you understand why we never met, why I didn't come to Rebekah and Jacob's funeral, and why I chose not to let you know about all of this until after I'm dead and buried.

I have more to say, but I want you to read Rebekah's letter first.

Chapter 7

Even though she'd only walked for a few minutes, Maggie turned off the treadmill and went to the living room. She was too restless to stay in any one spot. Keeping her place in the journal, she switched on a lamp and sat on the couch. She slowly turned the next page. A heavily creased envelope fell onto her lap. She picked it up and flipped it over, quickly drawing a sharp breath in as she saw her mother's handwriting. Tears welled in her eyes as she tried to swallow down the lump forming in her throat. Maggie was about to "hear" her mother's voice again, after all these years.

Mom,

I really don't know how to begin this letter. I never thought I'd write you or talk to you again. I received your letters. The petty part of me wants to say that I didn't even read them, but I did. So I know about Dad's passing. I wasn't sad when I read that he'd died. I felt relief, like I was finally able to turn the page and finish a horrible chapter in my life.

From what I gather in your letters, you think that since he's gone, you and I can now have a relationship again. Mom, we can't. You also played a huge role in all of this. It wasn't just Dad. You never protected me from him. You abandoned me, too, when I was at my most vulnerable and needed my mother. I don't think I can ever forgive you for that or let it go. And I have tried.

I feel terrible about the life and marriage you had, but Mom, you chose to stay with Dad. You chose to never stand up to him. You chose to appease Dad rather than choosing to protect me, your daughter. Honestly, you always acted more like my sister than my mother. It was like Dad was in charge of both of "us girls." But you were an adult; I was a helpless child. You were my mom, and you should have done everything in your power to protect me. That's what I would do for my daughter.

I think that's what I'm struggling with the most now. Becoming a mom has made it even harder for me to understand your lack of care for me. I'd never let anyone—my husband included—treat my little girl the way you allowed me to be treated. No, like you allowed me to be abused.

Mom, I want all of that to stay in my past. I don't want my

daughter to know about any of it. I mean, what would I say to her? What if, in explaining what happened, she thought she was the reason for . . . all of it? She's not. She's the biggest blessing I've ever been given, and as her mother, I will do anything to protect her—physically, emotionally, and mentally.

I decided years ago that I would never allow her to meet you or Dad, and not just because of what happened. I don't want her around your weird religious beliefs. You and Dad did not teach me the truth about God or the Bible. When Jacob's parents took me in, I started going to church with them. I was finally taught who and how God really is. Mom, He's loving. He's forgiving. He's good. He's just. I don't know if you still believe all the weirdness that you and Dad taught me, but I really hope you don't.

When my daughter was around four years old, she asked me about my mom and dad. I told her that my parents died when she was in my tummy because, Mom, that's the truth. My relationship with you and Dad died the day I told you I was pregnant. I know I got things out of order, and that getting pregnant disappointed and embarrassed Dad and you, but God allowed that whole situation to save me in every possible way. I could tell you so much more, but I don't want to. I don't want to give you more information about me, Jacob, our daughter, or our lives because you didn't earn it.

Mom, I don't wish you any ill will. I want you to finally be *happy. I want you to know the real God, and I want you to be free to live your life. But I don't want us to be a part of each other's lives. Please do not contact us again. This is your opportunity to be a good mother to me by finally doing what's best for me, and what's best for me is for you to stay in my past.*

Rebekah

Maggie closed the letter and slid it back into the envelope. She shut her eyes and sat motionless. Her mind was too full. Seeing her mom's handwriting, "hearing" her voice, and reading her innermost thoughts made her miss her mom with the same ache she had when her mom and dad first left. She felt the heavy, familiar weight of grief sitting on her chest again, smothering her. But at the same time, reading how much her mom truly loved and protected her made her feel so cared for, so fortunate.

She returned the envelope to the journal and shut the book. Then she went back to her bedroom, set the journal on her nightstand, and glanced at the clock—2:23 a.m.

Maggie got into bed, knowing she wouldn't be able to fall asleep, but her brain could not absorb any more information. She turned off her lamp and lay in the dark for a long time before finally drifting off to sleep.

Chapter 8

Maggie awoke to her phone vibrating on her nightstand.

She'd forgotten to turn off her weekday alarm—7:00 a.m.

She swung her legs off the bed, picked up her grandma's journal, and took it into the bathroom with her. She placed it on the counter and started her morning routine. When she finished, she picked up the journal, carried it into the kitchen, and set it on the island. She didn't really feel hungry. What she did feel was restless. Picking up the journal again, she took it into the next room and stepped onto the treadmill, setting it to a low speed.

Taking a deep breath through her nose, she blew the air out of her mouth before opening the book.

So, as you see, Magnolia, I didn't contact you because I was doing what your mom wanted me to do.

Her letter was very hard for me to read, but what she wrote was true. I had failed her as a mother. I wish so much that I could go back and do things differently. I know now, with Rodney being gone and all, how much calmer and happier my life could have been . . . how much better Rebekah's childhood could have been. I should have left Rodney or at least stood up to him. I should have protected Rebekah. I have a lot of "should haves."

I'm so glad that Rebekah seems to have been a good mom to you. She obviously didn't learn that from me. I think she must have tried to give you everything she didn't have, and I hope you had a wonderful childhood. I wish I could have been part of it, but the fact that I wasn't is my and Rodney's fault—not your mom's, and certainly not yours.

I know I wasn't any help in your childhood, but I hope I can be of some help in your future. If you're reading this, that means I've passed, and everything I own is now yours. Please do whatever you'd like with all of it—live in my house, sell my house, keep my things, sell my things. Whatever you want to do with it all is fine with me. I hope I'm leaving you a blessing and not a ton of work. I try to be tidy and keep my things in order. I kept everything of your mother's from when she was young. I hope you enjoy looking through those items and pictures.

Before I finish, I want to tell you something that you may not know. Did your mom ever tell you where your name came from? If not, let me. In my front yard is a large, beautiful magnolia tree. That was your mom's favorite place. She'd sit in that tree for hours—reading books, writing in her notebook, drawing, and so on. I have a picture now in her old bedroom of her sitting in that tree and reading. When she was little, I'd sometimes hear her talking to Magnolia—that's what she called the tree. One day, after she'd had a bath, I was brushing her hair—she was probably eight or nine—and she told me that someday, she'd have a little girl and name her Magnolia.

And she did.

Maggie stopped the treadmill and stepped off. She remembered asking her mom once why she'd named her Magnolia, and her mom had said, "I just always loved that name." Maggie didn't know about the tree in the front yard. She hadn't noticed it yesterday. She ached to see the tree and the picture of her mom as a little girl, sitting in Magnolia.

She rushed into her bedroom, journal in hand, and

grabbed her suitcase from the closet. Why? She had no idea. She could make the three-hour drive there and back in one day—as she'd done yesterday—but for some reason, she felt the need to prepare for staying the night. Maggie wanted to look through everything related to her mom: her calligraphy wall art, the photo of her in the magnolia tree, the piano where she'd learned to play.

Maggie missed her mom. She missed both of her parents, of course, but the opportunity to "meet" her mom as a little girl and to "spend time" with her again was too compelling. She had to get there as soon as possible.

Maggie threw everything she could possibly think of needing into her suitcase. After putting on a comfy outfit, she grabbed a blanket from her closet and her pillow from her bed. She plopped the blanket into her suitcase, carefully laid the journal on top, and closed the case.

If she got to her grandma's house and did decide to stay the night, she'd call her boss, letting her know that she needed to take some of her vacation days. Maggie was a hard-working, dependable employee, and her boss was always understanding, so it shouldn't be a problem.

Maggie put her suitcase in the trunk and set her pillow in the back seat. She usually listened to music or audiobooks during long drives, but today, she drove the entire way in silence. Well, her car was silent, but her thoughts were loud.

Was my grandma a good person?

Was Mom right or wrong to keep so many secrets from me . . . to lie to me?

What am I going to find inside that house?

Chapter 9

Maggie slowed the car as she pulled up to her grandmother's house and into the driveway. There was the magnolia tree—her mother's magnolia tree. It was huge and right next to the road. How had she missed it yesterday? It was almost growing *into* the road.

She parked in the driveway, got out, and walked over to the large tree. She put her hand on the trunk. As she did, a loud semitruck drove past, the wind from it blowing Maggie's long brown hair into her face.

The tree is gorgeous, thought Maggie as she tucked her hair behind her ears. *But how did Mom ever find any peace sitting out here right next to the road?*

Maggie went back to her car and got her things. Once on the porch, she inserted her newly owned key into the front door's lock but hesitated to turn it.

"Here we go," she said softly to herself as she turned the key and opened the door.

She slowly stepped inside, closed the door, and flicked on the light switch to her right. She was standing in a small foyer area with a coat rack to her left and wooden stairs leading to the second story in front of her. To her right was the family room, which connected to the kitchen. The air smelled faintly of lemon-scented cleaner. Thankfully, things looked tidy.

Maggie stepped into the family room. There was a brown tweed-looking fabric couch, a coffee table, a wooden rocking chair, and a dark green armchair. There was no TV. On the same wall as the stairs was an upright piano. Maggie set her suitcase down, then placed her purse on the coffee table and her pillow on the couch as she walked over to the piano. She stood beside it for a moment before pulling out the bench and sitting down.

Mom learned to play on this piano.

She put her right hand on the keys and played a few notes. Her left hand joined her right as she played "Oceans"—one of her mom's favorite songs. Maggie's mom had also taught her to play the piano, just as Rebekah's mom had taught her.

Emotions prevented Maggie from making it through the first chorus. She wiped her eyes as she looked at the items sitting on top of the piano. There was a lamp, an empty vase, and a decorative bowl filled with seashells.

Maggie walked into the kitchen. The cabinets, sink, and oven formed a horseshoe shape, with a small wooden table for four in the middle. The cabinets were honey oak, the counters were white Formica, and the floor was beige linoleum. There was no dishwasher. The window above the sink had a short, dark green curtain. The fridge was on the fourth wall, along with a door she assumed led out to the backyard. There were no dirty dishes in the sink.

Maggie turned to the refrigerator.

Oh dear, how many days ago did she die?

Bracing herself, she opened the fridge, only to find it completely empty.

Did someone come in and clean after she died? Or did she just . . . not eat?

She walked back through the family room and headed upstairs. She climbed slowly, looking at old photos hanging in the stairwell. Her phone rang from her pocket. She glanced at the screen before answering. It was Hadley.

"Hey," she answered, gazing at a black-and-white photo of an elderly couple in an oval frame.

"Hey, just wanted to check on you during my lunch break. How ya doing?"

"I'm good. Actually, I'm at my grandma's house. That feels so weird to say."

"You went back?"

"Yeah, I wanted to see some of the things she wrote about in her journal. I'm looking at photos now. The people in these pictures are probably all my relatives, and I have no idea who they are and have no one to ask. I mean . . . wait—" Maggie paused when she came to a photo of a young girl with a man and a woman. She immediately knew who the girl was.

"Mom—" she whispered.

"What?"

"Oh, umm, nothing. Let me let ya go now. I'll call tonight and fill you in."

"You okay?"

"Yeah, I'm fine—promise."

"Okay. I'll talk to you later."

"Bye."

Maggie leaned forward to examine the picture more closely. It looked like a church directory photo, taken in front of a marbled backdrop. Her mom appeared to be around ten years old. She had long brown hair with the front pulled back. The dress she wore had a huge, doily-like collar. She was smiling, but Maggie saw that her mom's eyes looked emotionless.

Her gaze shifted to the woman in the photo.

This must be my grandma Edith.

Edith was posed on the side of her daughter, her hands resting on Rebekah's shoulder. She also had on a dress with a large collar. Her brown hair was long, almost reaching her hips, with the front pulled back. She didn't have any makeup on. Her lips had a slight smile, and—like Maggie's mom—her eyes looked dead.

Maggie scowled at the man in the photo.

So, you're Rodney.

He looked arrogant—maybe because of what she knew of him, or maybe he really did appear that way, but either way, Maggie didn't like what she saw. He stood on the other side of Rebekah, wearing a plaid button-up shirt with his hands in the pockets of his khaki pants.

The remainder of the photos in the stairwell were filled with faces Maggie, of course, didn't recognize. There was a photo of a baby, but she couldn't tell whether it was her mother.

At the top of the stairs, Maggie found two bedrooms and a bathroom. She glanced first into the room on the left. Like the rest of the house, it was clean and tidy. There was a patchwork quilt on the double bed, along with a dresser, a nightstand, and a full-length freestanding mirror in the corner. On the nightstand, Maggie saw an alarm clock, a lamp, and two books. She walked over and picked up the books—one was the Bible, and the other was a book on the mysteries of ancient Egypt.

Maggie passed the hall bathroom on her way to the other bedroom.

She suddenly stopped walking and gasped.

Chapter 10

This had obviously been her mother's room.

The first thing Maggie's eyes focused on was the framed picture on the nightstand. It was a photo of Rebekah sitting in the magnolia tree, reading a book.

She walked over and gently sat on the edge of the twin bed. Picking up the frame, she studied the photo. Rebekah's hair was styled in two long braids. Maggie tried to figure out what book her mom was holding in the photo, but she couldn't tell. Her mom looked younger in this picture than in the stairwell family portrait, and her eyes appeared genuinely happy.

Maggie rested the frame on her lap as she looked up at the wall across from her. Hanging above the dresser was a framed Bible verse written in calligraphy. She hopped up to take a closer look. *"For I know the plans I have for you," declares* the Lord, *"plans to prosper you and not to harm you, plans to give you hope and a future." Jeremiah 29:11* was written in beautiful script.

Is this Mom's calligraphy piece?

Maggie set the photo of her mom on the dresser and carefully removed the frame from the wall. She turned it over to see if anything was written on the back. Nothing. After returning it to the wall, she stepped back and looked around the room slowly. Like her grandmother's, this bed also had a patchwork quilt.

Did my grandma make these blankets?

Did Mom help her?

Sadness washed over Maggie.

There was no way to know and no one to ask.

A well-loved brown teddy bear with a red ribbon around its neck was seated on top of the bed's pillow. Maggie picked it up and hugged it to her chest.

The room began to suffocate her.

She quickly laid the bear back on the bed and rushed downstairs to get some fresh air. Stepping onto the front porch, she closed her eyes and took some slow breaths in and out. When her chest felt less tight and her heart rate had slowed, she opened her eyes and was greeted by her mother's magnolia tree. She approached the tree and rested her hand where her mother was sitting in the photo.

Maggie's emotions were raw. She felt both closer to and more distant from her mother than she had in a long time.

Turning to lean against the tree, her eye caught a face in the neighbor's window—only for a brief moment before the curtain quickly closed. She jerked her head in the opposite direction.

Great. I'm being watched by the nosy neighbor.

As Maggie looked toward the road, she noticed her grandma's mailbox.

Wonder if there's any mail. Guess I should check.

She walked over to the mailbox and found a few letters inside. Gathering them up, she headed back to the house, flipping through the envelopes as she went. There was some junk mail, a bill, and a letter from the Newton County Road Department.

I'll open these later.

Maggie tossed them onto the coffee table. As they landed, she noticed that the coffee table had two drawers. She slid open the one closest to her and found three small photo albums inside.

Gathering the albums in her hands, she took them to the couch. After sitting down, she opened the light grey album first. The opening page read: Destin, Florida – 2024.

Most of the pictures inside were of beach sunsets and close-ups of various flowers, but there were two photos in the set of three elderly ladies. In one picture, the ladies were sitting on a bench in front of a restaurant. In the other, they stood on a boardwalk with the ocean in the background. Maggie studied their faces. The lady with shoulder-length dark gray hair favored the lady in the family photo from the stairwell, but in this photo, she looked happy. She had a real smile.

Maggie's mom had the same mouth shape when she smiled.

She picked up the next album. It was brown, and from the visible wear, it appeared to be the oldest of the three. When she opened it, she saw the word "Family" written on the inside cover. The penmanship was the same as the writing in her grandmother's journal. The photos in this album were small squares, each with a yellowish tint. The clothing and hairstyles in the pictures screamed that they were taken in the 1970s.

Maggie flipped through the pages of Christmas photos and what looked like family reunions. There was a young girl in the pictures who grew into an older teenager by the end of the album. She stood out to Maggie because her features favored her mom's—they had the same smile.

She closed the album and picked up the last one. It was a tan color. She opened the book, and written on the inside cover—in the same penmanship as the last album—was one word: Rebekah.

The first photo was of an adorable baby. Rebekah had a bald head and the biggest eyes. She was lying on a blanket on the floor in the family room—the same room Maggie was sitting in now. The furniture and layout hadn't changed.

The next picture was the same photo from the stairwell. Rebekah's hair had grown in a little, and she was sitting up on the couch. She was wearing a white dress with tiny purple flowers on it.

Maggie slowly took in every photo as she watched her mom grow up right before her eyes. She had always known she favored her mom—same brown hair, same nose shape, same smile—but seeing these pictures made Maggie realize just how much they *really* resembled each other. The only visual characteristics she and her mom didn't share were their eye color and height. Maggie had inherited her dad's blue eyes and some of his stature. Her dad was six feet tall, while her mom had been five foot four. Maggie was three inches taller than her mom.

There were only about thirty pictures in Rebekah's album. There were photos of Rebekah holding her teddy bear, playing piano, baking a cake, threading a sewing machine, and sitting in Magnolia. There weren't any photos of Rebekah and Edith together except for one. It was of Edith holding Rebekah—who looked to be around three or four years old—outside a church. A man who resembled the man in the stairwell family photo was in the background, talking to two other men.

I guess old Rodney never took photos of them. I bet Grandma was the one who took every one of these pictures of Mom.

Maggie placed the photo albums on the coffee table next to the small stack of mail. She went upstairs and brought down the teddy bear, the photo of her mom sitting in Magnolia, and the calligraphy Bible verse. She set the three items on the coffee table alongside the albums.

What else do I want to keep?

She looked around the house. Her stomach interrupted her thoughts with a loud rumble. Pulling her phone out of her pocket, she looked at the time—almost three o'clock. She hadn't eaten breakfast or lunch.

Maggie had passed a grocery store a few miles up the road on her way to her grandma's house. She decided to pick up some food, come back to the house to eat, and then go through the rest of the house to see if there were any other keepsakes she wanted to take with her.

Before heading to the store, she called her boss and asked to use some of her vacation time. It was no problem for her to take the rest of the week off. She'd need to leave by Friday evening so she'd be home to visit her grandpa on Saturday.

Chapter 11

Maggie slowly rolled over, covering her face with her blanket to block out the morning sun shining through the crack in the curtains. She'd stayed up past midnight, rummaging through drawers and cabinets. She almost went up to the attic to search around, but Hadley had turned that idea into a scary movie scene when they were on the phone last night. Maggie decided that searching the dark attic with its squeaky pull-down ladder could wait until daylight.

Maggie had slept on the couch. She'd found a sheet in the upstairs bathroom closet and used it to cover the couch cushions. She'd changed into her pajamas before lying down with her pillow and blanket.

"Rrrrrrrr!"

Maggie jerked up to a seated position.

What on earth was that?

The deafening noise filled the room again.

She jumped off the couch and ran to the front window of the family room. Yanking the curtain aside, she saw men wearing hard hats and two trucks in her driveway. One of the men was up in her mother's magnolia tree, cutting down the branches with a chainsaw. Another man was pulling the branches to the side, where another worker was sawing the branches into smaller logs.

"What?" Maggie yelled.

Without putting on her shoes, she ran out the front door and straight to the man closest to her. He was sitting in the passenger seat of one of the trucks with the door open.

"What are you doing?" Maggie screamed over the sounds.

He was wearing large headphones and couldn't hear her.

She touched him on his arm, causing him to jump. He quickly uncovered his ears, stepped out of the truck, and stood next to the door. He glanced at her face and then stared down to the side.

"What are you all doing?" Maggie yelled again.

"We're—we're cutting down this tree."

"*What*? You can't cut down this tree! This was my *mom*'s tree! This—" she largely motioned to the tree, "this is *Magnolia*! You can't just show up here and start cutting down my tree! Who on earth do you—"

"You are talking too much," the man stated. Then he put on his headphones, sat back in the truck, and closed the door.

Maggie's mouth was agape. "Wh-what?" she shrieked. "How dare you—"

"Ma'am? Ma'am? Can I help you?"

She turned to see another man jogging toward her.

"Help me?" she shouted. "Yeah, you can stop cutting down my tree! This—this is my *mother*'s magnolia tree!"

"We were hired by the county, ma'am. They send out letters notifying homeowners before we come. The tree is too close to the new road. It has to come down for safety reasons."

To Maggie's surprise and embarrassment, tears were rolling down her cheeks. "But . . . but you . . . you can't cut her down. This tree . . . it's—"

Maggie felt a hand on her shoulder. She spun around to see a short, little elderly woman with pure white hair. The lady looked familiar.

"Come with me, dear. You just come with me, and I'll explain everything," said the woman. "I've got her, Joel. She'll be fine." The lady looked again at Maggie. "Come on, dear." She placed her hand on Maggie's back.

Maggie blindly went with the woman—maybe because she realized she was standing in front of a group of men, barefoot, in her pajamas, with crazy hair, screaming, and crying, or maybe because the words "I'll explain everything" felt too enticing. Maggie had been overwhelmed with confusion for almost four straight days now, and explanations were exactly what she craved.

"You just come with me. You come with Sage, and we'll have a talk," said the lady as she walked arm in arm with Maggie.

"Sage?" Maggie asked as she wiped her eyes with her free hand. They walked over to the house next door.

You're the nosy neighbor!

"That's me. My name is Sage," the woman answered cheerfully. "And you are Magnolia." Sage opened her front door and motioned for Maggie to come in.

Maggie slowly stepped inside, greeted by the glorious smell of coffee. Sage closed the door and led her into the dining room.

Sage was clearly a beach lover. Her home was filled with coastal-themed décor.

"Right this way, dear. Let's sit and talk while we have some breakfast. Have you eaten yet?"

"No, ma'am," Maggie replied as she sat in the dining chair Sage pulled out for her. Maggie caught her reflection in the mirrors of Sage's china cabinet. She looked a fright. "I'm so sorry for how I look," she said, smoothing the top of her hair and tucking strands behind her ears. "I feel . . . I feel completely out of sorts."

"No apologies needed! You've been through a lot these last few days, and then to wake up to Magnolia being cut down . . . Well, that had to be a rude awakening." Sage disappeared into the next room and then reappeared with a coffee pot and two cups. "Coffee, dear?"

"Yes, please. You . . . called the tree Magnolia."

"Well, that's its name. Your mother named it, right?" Sage asked as she filled Maggie's cup.

Maggie stared at her. "Did—did you know my mom?"

"No, dear, but I feel like I did from everything your grandmother told me." Sage turned and went back into the kitchen. She returned to the table with a sugar dish and a bottle of creamer. "I've been looking forward to meeting you. I hate that it had to be under these circumstances, but I knew that if I ever *did* get to meet you . . . well, this would be how it had to be. Do you like bacon and scrambled eggs?"

"Oh, yes. I do." Maggie smiled. "Very much."

"Bacon and eggs it is, then! I'll get to cooking, and you just catch your breath here. The restroom is right through there if you need it," said Sage as she motioned to the door on her left. Then she headed back to the kitchen, calling out, "This won't take long. Make yourself at home!"

"Thank you." Maggie watched her leave the room.

Sage was a petite woman—maybe five feet one. Even early in the morning, she already looked very put together. She had on pink-and-white plaid capris, a pink blouse, and matching bright pink lipstick. Her white hair was cut in a chic pageboy. Not many women could pull off that look well, but Sage did. She wore pearl earrings and a pearl necklace.

Maggie glanced at her reflection in the china cabinet again. She got up and walked to the restroom. It smelled like lemons—the same scent as her grandma's house. After closing the door and turning on the light, Maggie got a clearer look at herself in the mirror.

Good heavens.

She pulled her fingers through her crazy hair and smoothed it as best as she could. The collar of her pajama shirt was sticking up on one side, so she flipped it back down to its rightful position. Then she straightened her pants, which had been twisted too far around her waist. Her face was red and splodgy from crying. She turned on the water, splashed some on her cheeks, and then patted her skin dry with the hand towel hanging nearby.

Returning to the table, Maggie added some creamer to her coffee and took a sip.

She felt a bit better.

After a minute, she stood up and walked in the direction Sage had gone. Around the corner of the dining room doorway, she found Sage cooking in the kitchen, wearing an apron covered in a seashell pattern.

"Mrs. Sage? I hope I've not messed up your morning plans."

"Oh no, dear. I had nothing planned, nothing at all. And call me Sage. Just Sage—that's what all my friends call me, and it's what I like being called the best."

"I don't think I've ever heard the name Sage before."

"Oh, good!" Sage looked back at Maggie and smiled. "I get to tell one of my favorite stories about two of my favorite people!" She turned back around and poured the scrambled eggs into a dish while she talked. "My sweet daddy was a chef—the best chef there ever was! And my momma was a master gardener, truly a *master* gardener. She grew all of the herbs that Daddy used at his restaurant."

She faced Maggie again. "Could you please grab the bowl

of raspberries out of the fridge?"

"Sure," Maggie answered.

"Gotta have our fiber! When you get to be my age, you *gotta* have your fiber!" Sage said with a laugh. She picked up a plate of bacon and the dish of eggs. "Can you also grab those plates and forks there?" She motioned with her head to the counter.

"Yes, ma'am." Maggie picked up the stacked plates with two napkins and forks on top.

"Just follow me," Sage sang as she walked back to the dining room. She placed the dishes of food on the table. "I'll be right back with our drinks. Would you like water or orange juice?"

"Water, please," said Maggie as she set out their plates, napkins, and forks.

Maggie sat down as Sage returned with two glasses of water. "If your coffee needs topping off, just let me know." Sage joined her at the table. "All righty then, let's pray." She lowered her head, and Maggie followed. "Dear Lord, we thank You for Your goodness. We thank You for this day and for this food. And I thank You, Father, for Magnolia. Please bless her and all that she does. Amen.

"You take as much as you'd like," Sage said as she handed Maggie the serving spoon from the dish of eggs. "Now, where was I? Oh yes, Momma and Daddy. They first got pregnant with my older sister. Now, they didn't know she was a girl at the time, of course. They didn't have all that ultrasound stuff back then. Well, they wanted to give their child a name that really meant something to both of them, not just sounded pretty. Daddy loved, loved, loved to cook, and Momma felt the same way about her gardening. So, they chose the names Basil if it was a boy and Rosemary if it was a girl."

Maggie ate while watching and listening to Sage. This little old lady spoke, moved, and did everything with such energy and enthusiasm. Maggie immediately liked her.

"So, Rosemary was born. Then I came along, and they named me Sage. Then our younger brother, Basil, joined us. Isn't that just wonderful? Rosemary, Sage, and Basil." Sage's eyes danced as she talked.

"It *is* wonderful," Maggie agreed.

Sage hopped out of her seat. "Let me show you a photo of Momma and Daddy." She took a silver frame from the middle of her china cabinet and handed it to Maggie. "Here they are right after they'd gotten married."

Maggie looked down at a black-and-white photo of a young couple, clearly in love. They were holding hands and standing on the front steps of a church.

"What a beautiful photo and what a good-looking couple," said Maggie as she handed the frame back.

"Yes, they were such a good-looking couple." Sage returned the frame to its shelf and sat back down. "So that's why I like for people to just call me Sage. I love my name—it makes me think of my momma and daddy. They've both been gone, well, let's see . . . Daddy passed in 2001, and Momma joined him in 2002. We knew she wouldn't stay with us long, not with Daddy not here and all. She wanted to be with him." Sage nodded at Maggie. "Oh my, listen to me, just jabbering. How's your food? You need anything?"

"It's all delicious. Thank you." Maggie shifted in her seat. "Sage, what did you mean when you said you'd explain everything?"

Chapter 12

Sage set her fork down. "I meant that I'll explain everything I can. I don't know it all, but I know a lot. First off, let's start with Magnolia. Last year, the state highway department started changing our two-lane road into a four-lane. We'd been getting so much traffic here lately that it really did need to be done. They recently finished it, and when they did, the new lane was almost touching Magnolia. I'm really surprised they didn't remove the tree before paving this section. So, Edith and I knew this was coming. I'm sorry that it was a surprise to you and that it happened while you were here."

"Were you close friends with my grandmother?"

"Oh, yes. Edith and I were two peas in a pod! We became friends almost fourteen years ago. See, my late husband, Henry, and I moved here in 2008, but Edith and I didn't buddy up until after Rodney died in 2010. We weren't *allowed* to be friends until then."

"Because of Rodney?"

Sage nodded.

"What was he like?" Maggie asked. "From what I read, he seemed pretty awful."

"Oh, he was worse than that! Rodney was a complete narcissist. Let me just tell you how we met him. Henry and I moved here from Florida, and I'm a sun-lover. We moved into this house in . . . July, and one Saturday, I set my lounger chair out in the backyard—in *our* backyard, mind you. I wanted to get some sun, so I was in my swimsuit. Well, while I was out there reading my magazine, Rodney apparently came by and knocked on the front door. Henry filled me in about it later that day. Rodney told Henry that he needed to"—she made air quotes—"'rein in his wife and make her put some clothes on.'"

"He did not!"

"He did too!"

"What did your husband do?" asked Maggie.

Sage leaned back, laughed, and slapped her knee. "He told Rodney to get off our property and warned him that if he ever came back, he'd punch him in the face! He'd have done it too! Now listen, Henry wasn't a violent man at all, but he didn't let anyone mess with me, our daughter, or our grandkids."

"Did Rodney ever come over again?"

"No, thankfully, never. We'd see him and Edith coming and going, and working in their yard, and so on, but we never spoke. Rodney always had an arrogant scowl on his face, and poor Edith always stared at the ground. I do re-member smiling and nodding at Edith once when we were both working in our gardens. She smiled back at me, prob-ably because Rodney was at work then and couldn't catch her interacting with the *heathen* neighbor!" Sage chuckled. "After Rodney died, Edith showed up one day on our front porch with some cucumbers—said she had more than she could use and wanted to give us some. And that started our friendship.”

“What was she like?”

“She was very quiet and reserved when I first met her. She’d been through a lot, beaten down for so long—emotionally and physically—by that narcissist. But after he died, she came out of her shell more and more. I remember she didn’t laugh much when we first started spending time together. It was almost as if she’d forgotten how. Honestly, I don’t know if she’d ever really felt the freedom to laugh and be truly happy before. But over the months, that changed. Edith’s jokes were my favorites because they were always unexpected. I think she’d been saving up her humor for so long that when she let it spill out, it was just the best!

“She never did wear pants or shorts, not even after Rodney died. Not that there’s anything wrong with skirts, but I don’t think there’s anything wrong with pants either. I asked her about it once, and she said she just didn’t feel comfortable in pants. I guess when you’ve worn nothing but skirts for around forty years, it’s hard to change. I did finally get her on board with wearing lipstick, but she’d only ever try natural shades—not like yours truly,” Sage said as she fluttered her eyelashes and puckered her lips.

Maggie grinned, but her smile slowly faded.

“You have something on your mind—I can tell,” said Sage. “You can just say it. I’m an open book, my dear.”

“The lawyer who gave me Grandma’s keys said her neighbor found her when she passed. Was that you?”

Sage nodded.

“I’m so sorry,” said Maggie.

“It was a shock.” Sage looked down and rubbed her hands on her knees, trying to keep herself from crying. “See, I’m eleven years older than Edith. I thought I’d surely go first, but God had different plans.”

Sage leaned back in her chair. "For the last few years, Edith and I ate lunch together every day. We'd take turns eating here one day and then at her house the next. It was her turn to come over for lunch, but she never showed up. I walked over to check on her when—when I saw her." Sage's eyes filled with tears. "The doctor said she'd died instantly, so—so there was no suffering." She wiped her eyes with her napkin, careful not to mess up her makeup.

"You were a good friend to her. I can tell."

Sage smiled. "We were good friends to each other. Edith was a blessing." She sniffed and shifted positions in her chair. "Now you said that the lawyer gave you her keys. Did he also give you your journal?"

Maggie paused. "Yes, ma'am. My grandma told you about it?"

"Oh, she let me read it when she finished writing it. There was a calm and peace in Edith after she wrote that journal that I hadn't seen in her before. I think it was an acceptance of how things were—an acceptance of her reality." Sage studied Maggie's face. "I'm sure reading it was a lot for you to take in."

"It was—it is."

Sage reached across the table and took Maggie's hand. "Edith had a lot of regrets, just like all of us. Some she was pushed into, but others she earned. Now, no person is all good or all bad—except for Rodney. He was pretty much *all* bad." She winked at Maggie and patted her hand. Sage leaned back in her seat. "Edith was my dear friend, and I loved her. I still do. She was very good to me, but I don't fault your mom for how she felt or for the decisions she made. Your mom did what she thought was best for you, and she allowed what she thought she could handle. None of us can judge anyone for how they handle things because we've never been in their shoes. People love to say things like, 'Well, I'd have done this' or 'She should have done that,' when honestly, none of us truly know what we'd do in a situation until we're in it."

Chapter 13

Maggie helped Sage clear the breakfast dishes from the table.

"So, what's on your docket for today?" Sage asked as she set their water glasses in the sink.

"I want to go through the attic and see what's up there. I've made a pile of things I'd like to keep, and that's the last place I've got to look through."

"Will you be heading back to your home after that?"

"No, I'll stay tonight, and then I'll head out in the morning."

"Would you like to come over for dinner tonight? I mean, I know you've already had a large helping of Sage," she said with a smile, "but I'd love to spend some more time with you before you leave."

Maggie felt tears welling in her eyes, but she held them back. She didn't understand why she was reacting this way to Sage's words. Was it because she'd been on her own for so long?

"I'd like that," said Maggie.

"Oh, good!" Sage grabbed both of Maggie's hands and did a little stomping dance. "I'll cook us a casserole and some vegetables, and do you like pecan pie or peach cobbler?"

Maggie's tears escaped. She smiled and cleared her throat. "Umm, peach cobbler."

"Cobbler it is! Five o'clock sound good?"

"Sounds perfect."

"Oh, and let me give you my number in case you need to reach me." Sage opened a drawer and pulled out a pen and a small notepad. After writing down her phone number, she ripped off the page and handed it to Maggie. "You call me anytime for anything."

"Thank you. I'll text you when I'm back with my phone so you'll have my number too.

Maggie folded the paper and slid it into the pocket of her pajama pants. "Well, I'd best get up to that attic and get to work. Thank you, Sage."

"You're welcome, dear," Sage replied as she walked with Maggie to her foyer. Before opening the front door, she paused and turned to face Maggie, putting a hand on each of Maggie's arms. "Okay, I haven't heard the chainsaws for a bit now, so I bet they've finished cutting Magnolia down. Are you ready to go outside?"

Maggie nodded.

"Big breath," said Sage, and they both inhaled and exhaled together.

Maggie smiled at her and nodded.

Sage opened the door.

She was right—Magnolia was gone. The men were loading the last logs onto a truck.

Maggie kept her head down and hurried back to her grandma's house.

Maggie pulled down the attic ladder. She turned on her phone's flashlight and climbed the rungs, stopping when her head reached above the attic's floor. The air was hot and muggy. Lifting her phone even with her head, she slowly shined the light around the dark attic. She saw a cardboard box labeled "Christmas Decorations" and a large steamer trunk. She waited for a moment before moving. Hadley's warning of spiders, snakes, and killers had made her feel a bit anxious. Thankfully, she didn't see anything move.

She climbed the rest of the way up and went over to the trunk. It looked old, made of wood and leather. The handles were worn, and the sides scraped, as if it had been on a grand adventure long ago. With growing excitement, she unhooked its latch, but that feeling quickly dissipated when she saw the inside was empty.

She moved over to the Christmas box and opened it. Inside, she found a wooden nativity set, a wreath, a small decorative canvas that read *"O, Come Let Us Adore Him,"* two dish towels covered in a poinsettia print, and a ceramic Christmas tree—the kind with real Christmas lights that worked.

Maggie smiled. She wanted to keep all of it.

She closed the box back up and carefully maneuvered it down the ladder.

Maggie set the box on the floor next to the coffee table, covered with keepsakes. She pulled her phone out of her pocket. After plopping down on the couch, she looked up estate sale companies in Newton County.

"Right on time!" said Sage as she opened the door.

Maggie smiled as she walked inside. "Oooo, something smells good."

"We're having us some chicken casserole, green beans, carrots, and peach cobbler with vanilla ice cream."

"That sounds perfect!"

Sage already had the dishes on the table. Maggie and Sage sat in the same spots as that morning.

Reaching for Maggie's glass, Sage asked, "Would you like water or tea?"

"Tea, please," Maggie answered.

Sage picked up one of the two pitchers on the table. She filled Maggie's glass and then her own.

"Well, let's thank the Lord and then dig in before it gets cold." Sage lowered her head. "Father, thank You for this food and this sweet time with my new friend, Magnolia. We love You, Lord. Amen." She raised her head and smiled. "Okay, let's eat! Just help yourself!"

Maggie spooned some chicken casserole onto her plate as Sage picked up the bowl of green beans.

"These here are your grandmother's green beans from her garden," Sage said as she put some on her own plate. "Edith and I always did our canning together, and then we'd share everything with each other. She was a wonderful gardener. Did you go out in the backyard today to see her garden?"

"No, I didn't. I was so focused on going through the house that I completely forgot about the backyard. I'll be sure to take a look tomorrow morning before I leave."

"So, what are your plans for the house?"

"I contacted two estate sale companies today. They're each going to send someone out to meet with me on Wednesday morning. They'll look through everything and give me their prices, the dates they have available, and all that info."

Sage nodded as she chewed.

"Would you like to go through the house before they come?" asked Maggie. "I'd be happy for you to take anything you want to keep."

"That's so sweet of you, Magnolia. Thank you. I might just do that. Oh, but before I forget—" She stood and took a key out of her pocket. "Let me give you this. It's an extra key to Edith's house. She and I traded extra keys years ago. I got my key from her house last week; I hope you don't mind that I let myself in to do that." She held the key out to Maggie.

"I don't mind at all, but could you hold onto Grandma's key a bit longer? Since I don't live here, I'd feel a lot better knowing you could get in next door if needed."

Sage smiled and nodded. "I can do that." She placed the key on the edge of her china cabinet.

"When you were at her house last week, did you happen to clean? When I walked in yesterday, it smelled like the same lemon cleaner fragrance as your bathroom. And the fridge had been cleaned out."

Sage nodded again as she chewed and swallowed. "I did. I knew you'd be going inside sooner or later, and I wanted it to be ready for you. Edith would have wanted that."

Maggie smiled. "Thank you. And thank you for this delicious meal. Everything tastes amazing."

Sage beamed. "You're so welcome! I love to cook, I love to eat, and I love having company."

After taking a drink of her tea, Sage asked, "So, you say you'll be back on Wednesday?"

"Yes, I'm supposed to meet the first estate sale person at 10:00 a.m. and the second person at 2:00 p.m."

"Is all of this messing you up at work? Where do you work?"

"No, the timing's actually as good as it could be. I'm a graphic designer at a marketing firm. I finished my part on a job this past Monday, so I'm not as pressed for time as I was even last week. And my boss is super understanding. She told me she'd work with me while I'm handling all of this."

"Good, that's good," said Sage. "Well, if you have time between the estate sale meetings, could you come over for lunch? Or for dinner that evening?"

"That sounds great! Let's do dinner so we won't be rushed at all."

"Perfect!"

Chapter 14

The next morning, Maggie took a shower, got ready, and packed all her keepsakes into her car. Before leaving, she went inside and walked through the house to the kitchen's back door. She wanted to keep her word to Sage and look at her grandma's garden. Unlocking the deadbolt, she opened the door and found a small wooden deck covered with potted plants. Most appeared to be herbs.

Maggie's eyes left the deck as she looked up to view the backyard. It was beautiful. The left side was covered with well-kept, tidy rows of vegetables. The right side contained fruit trees and gorgeous flowers. Two fig trees caught Maggie's eye. Her mom had always made the best fig preserves. When she was a teenager, Rebekah taught her how to make the delicious jam.

Maggie stepped back into the kitchen. When she'd gone

on her keepsake hunting mission Wednesday night, she'd found some baskets in one of the lower kitchen cabinets. She opened the cabinet and took out a basket.

Returning to the yard, Maggie picked most of the ripe figs from the trees, stopping only when her basket was full. As she walked back, she looked over at Sage's house. She spotted Sage peering through one of the back windows, a huge smile on her face. She waved enthusiastically. Maggie held up the basket filled with figs and grinned. Sage clapped her hands and then gave Maggie a thumbs-up.

Maggie locked up the house and got into her car. She placed the basket of figs on her passenger seat. While fastening her seatbelt, her phone rang—it was Hadley.

"Hey," Maggie said as she pulled out of the driveway.

"Headed home?"

"Leaving right now, and guess what I have sitting next to me?"

"What?"

"A basket full of figs."

Hadley gasped. "Fig preserves, please!"

"You got it!"

Since becoming friends, Maggie had given Hadley a jar of her homemade fig preserves as part of every Christmas gift.

"Yay! So, anything new to tell me? Did you go through the haunted attic? Did you find a trunk filled with treasure?"

"Well, it's definitely not haunted, but I did find a trunk!"

"Filled with gold?"

Maggie laughed. "I wish! No, it was empty."

"Boring," Hadley sang.

Maggie saw a sign reading "Tina's Diner" coming up on the right side of the road. It was almost noon, and she hadn't eaten breakfast that morning.

"Hey, let me call you back. I'm going to stop and eat some lunch real quick."

"Sounds good. Talk to you later."

"Bye."

Maggie pulled into the small but packed parking lot, taking the last available spot.

Place must be good, she thought as she got out of her car.

Walking into the diner, she was immediately greeted by the lively sounds of conversation, laughter, and dishes being set on tables. It smelled great inside. A middle-aged waitress carrying a full tray stopped in front of her and smiled.

"Welcome to Tina's. You can have a seat right there, sweetie," she said, motioning with her head to an empty table. "I'll be right with you."

"Thank you." Maggie slid into the booth.

A minute later, the waitress was back with a menu. "Okay, now, what can I get you to drink?"

"Water and a coffee, please."

"You got it! I'll be right back with those, and I'll get your order."

Maggie studied the menu. The meatloaf plate with mashed potatoes and macaroni and cheese sounded perfect.

"Okay, here we go," said the waitress as she set the coffee mug and glass of water on the table. "Creamer and sugar are there. Now, what can I get you?"

"I'd like the meatloaf with mashed potatoes and macaroni and cheese, please."

"That's my favorite! Good choice. I'll have it out to you soon." The waitress collected Maggie's menu and headed to the kitchen.

Maggie could tell this place ran like a well-oiled machine. Even though it was packed and loud, the waitresses all seemed calm and cheerful. Her eyes scanned the room, taking in all the people, until her gaze stopped on two men sitting at a booth against the far wall. One man was the rude headphone-wearing truck guy, and the other was the man Sage had called Joel.

Maggie looked down as her face immediately flushed from embarrassment and anger. She was mortified by her display yesterday morning and still slightly fuming over the guy who told her she talked too much.

Please, God, don't let them see me.

Her thoughts were interrupted when the waitress set her plate down.

"Here ya go!"

"Oh, that was fast! Thank you."

Maggie wished she'd brought in a book or something to keep her eyes occupied while she ate. That way, there'd be no chance of her making eye contact with either of the two tree men.

She picked up her napkin and unwrapped it from her silverware.

"That looks gross."

Maggie's head jerked up to see headphone man standing at her table. She stared at his face, but he never looked at her. He kept his eyes on her plate.

"You should've gotten chicken fingers and tater tots. They taste good."

His expression didn't change as he spoke.

"Owen? Oh, there you are!" Joel came up beside headphone guy, then glanced down at Maggie. "Oh—hello."

"Hi," said Maggie.

Joel turned back to Owen. "I got up to talk to Mr. Jones, and you disappeared." He looked again at Maggie. "How are you today, ma'am?"

"I'm—I'm better," she answered sheepishly.

"Oh, there's Owen and Joel!" said a short, chubby lady as she approached, her husband walking behind her.

Maggie watched as Joel and Owen both turned toward them, Joel with a smile on his face and Owen's expression unchanged. Owen stared down to the side.

"Well, hey there!" said Joel as he shook the man's hand.

"You getting some more fried chicken?"

The man and Joel both laughed.

"Oh, no, no. I got more than I should've last night. We just came by to get some take-out because—" The man stopped speaking and playfully nudged his wife.

"That's right, Owen doesn't know yet," she said to her husband. "Owen, guess what we have waiting on us in a box in the truck?"

Owen turned his head more toward the woman but kept his eyes down. "Puppies?" he asked, his tone unchanging. "Did Penny have her puppies?"

The woman laughed. "You guessed it, Owen! She did!"

Owen rocked side to side and flapped his hands as he stared at the ground.

"Six puppies," she continued. "We just took them to the vet for a checkup. Wanna come out and see 'em?" She cut her eyes to Joel and whispered, "Would that be okay?"

Joel smiled and nodded. "Owen, you go on out with Mrs. Julia while I pay."

Without a word, Owen headed for the door, Julia following him.

"And I'd best get our food," said Julia's husband. He smiled and nodded at Maggie before patting Joel on the shoulder on his way to the counter.

Joel looked back down at Maggie. Her embarrassment and definitely her rage had vanished. For the first time, she noticed his soft blue eyes and long eyelashes.

"Owen's my brother. I—I hope he didn't say anything that upset you yesterday."

"Oh, no. No, he didn't."

Joel's shoulders relaxed. "That's good. We're both sorry about your grandmother. She was a nice lady."

"You knew my grandma?"

"Yeah, we went to church together—my family, your grandma, Sage," he nodded toward Julia's husband, "Burt and Julia." His eyes returned to Maggie's. "And I'm sorry about cutting down her tree."

"Oh, no apology needed. I'm sorry for coming out all crazy-like yesterday. I was just . . . surprised . . . and sad."

He sympathetically nodded. "I bet you've got a lot of work to do over at Mrs. Edith's house, and you probably don't know anyone here in town. Do you?"

"Well, I know Sage now."

Joel grinned. "Sage—now, she's a character."

"She definitely is, and I already love her."

"Listen, if you need any help at the house with . . . anything, just let me know." He reached into his back pocket and pulled out his wallet. He opened it, took out a business card, and handed it to Maggie. "I'm Joel. Here's my cell number. Don't hesitate to give me a call if I can help in any way."

"Thank you." Maggie accepted the card. "That's very thoughtful."

"Well, I don't wanna make your food any colder." He smiled.

Beautiful teeth.

"Hope you have a great day," he said.

"You too, and thank you again."

As Joel left the diner, Maggie studied his card—Barrett Tree Service, Joel Barrett.

Chapter 15

Back at her apartment, Maggie spent the remainder of the day unpacking keepsakes and making fig preserves. The air around her was thick with memories. She'd felt the heaviness of missing her mom—missing *both* of her parents—all week, and emotionally, she was exhausted. After dinner, she lay on the couch with her phone so she could mindlessly scroll for a bit, but she fell asleep after only a couple of minutes. She didn't wake up until late the next morning.

After showering, she made biscuits and ate one with her fig preserves for breakfast. Before cleaning the kitchen, she split another biscuit open, spooned preserves onto one half, closed the biscuit back up, and wrapped it in foil. She placed it and a jar of unopened preserves on the edge of the counter and went to finish getting ready for the day.

Maggie pulled into the parking lot of the memory care facility where her grandpa lived. She went inside, grabbed her visitor sticker, and headed to her grandpa's room. Leaning her head inside, she tapped on his open door.

"Knock, knock," said Maggie.

"Hello there, Ms. Maggie! Good morning!" Patricia was brushing her grandpa's hair. "Mr. Liam, you've got company. Maggie is here to see you."

Liam raised his head and smiled. "Good morning."

"Good morning," Maggie said as she set her purse on top of his dresser.

"Well, I'll just leave you two to have some visitin' time together," said Patricia as she set the hairbrush on the dresser next to Maggie's purse. Liam didn't have much hair left, but Patricia made sure that his few wisps on top always started off the day in place.

Maggie pulled a jar of preserves out of her purse.

"These are for you," she said, handing the jar to Patricia. "Fig preserves—I made them last night."

Patricia took the jar and was about to thank Maggie when Liam said, "Fig preserves? Those were our Rebekah's favorite. You always liked them, too, Maggie."

Maggie looked wide-eyed at Patricia.

Alzheimer's is both cruel and gracious, Patricia had told Maggie on the first day she placed her grandpa in the facility. *It takes our loved ones away from us, and then every once in a while, out of nowhere, it allows them to come back. And there's nothin' sweeter than those brief moments.*

Patricia closed her eyes, breathed in and out, and slowly

shook her head. Opening her eyes, she whispered, "Nothin' sweeter." She held up the jar of preserves and mouthed the words "thank you" to Maggie before quietly stepping out into the hall.

Maggie swallowed down the lump in her throat and took the foil-wrapped biscuit from her purse.

"Grandpa, I made you a biscuit with fig preserves. Would you like to eat it now?" she asked, sitting down beside him.

"Ooh now, I'm not gonna pass that up, Maggie-Girl."

He's back.

Maggie quickly unwrapped the biscuit and handed it to him.

He took a bite and smiled while he chewed. "Rebekah taught you well. These taste just like hers."

"I made them with figs from the house where Mom grew up. I was at Edith Patton's home this week."

His smile vanished. "You were with Edith?" He leaned forward. "Was Rodney there?"

"No, no. Rodney died in 2011 or 2012, and Edith passed away just a couple weeks ago. I was at their house, getting it ready for an estate sale."

He relaxed and took another bite.

"Grandpa, did you . . . did you ever meet Edith or Rodney?"

He swallowed. "No, thankfully. Rebekah didn't want us to have anything to do with them, and from what she told us, I can't say I blame her. I tried to step in and be as much of a father figure as I could, and your grandma"—Maggie knew he meant his wife—her grandma Jane—"tried to be a good mom to Rebekah."

He took another bite, and as he chewed, he glanced back at his door. Turning again to Maggie, he asked, "Hey, when are Jacob and Rebekah coming by to see me?"

He's leaving me again.

Maggie tried to keep the sorrow from showing on her face. "I bet they're coming to visit you tomorrow."

Wednesday morning, Maggie pulled into the driveway of her newly acquired house. There was a shirtless young man—a very *good-looking* shirtless young man—mowing the grass in her front yard. Seeing her get out of her car and walk toward him, he stopped his mower.

"Hi, umm, I'm not sure who you are, but this is my property," she said, motioning to the house.

"Oh, you're Magnolia." He grinned as he took off his sunglasses. "I'm Dylan—Sage's grandson. I've mowed my grandma's and Mrs. Edith's yards for years. Grandma asked me to keep mowing over here until you get the house sold."

"Thank you, that's very kind," Maggie said, smiling as she smoothed her hair behind her ear.

Dylan was muscular and tan. His blond hair showed at the sides and back of his ball cap.

"Need help taking anything inside?" he asked as he wiped sweat from his face with a bandana he'd taken from his pocket.

"No, no, I didn't bring much with me. Thank you, though."

"No problem. I'll just get back to it, then. Good to meet you." He smiled, winked at her, and started the mower.

Maggie turned to head back to her car, suddenly very aware of how she was walking.

Did he wink at me? It was a small wink, but definitely a wink!

She pulled her suitcase out of the trunk and went inside, glancing once at Dylan as she walked.

At ten o'clock, the first estate sale representative arrived. Maggie walked her through the house, showing her everything. She liked the information the woman gave her for the sale, but she didn't like the woman—she was snooty.

At two o'clock, a middle-aged man came from the other estate company. Maggie immediately liked him. He was very knowledgeable about estate sales and had good tips, like the other lady, but he was also cheerful and kind.

"Your grandma took care of what she had, Ms. Maggie, and that really helps with selling it all. I don't think you'll have any trouble emptying the house, and we'd sure be happy to help you with that."

"Thank you, Mr. Turner." Maggie looked down at the paperwork he'd given her when he arrived. "Let me grab a pen, and I'll get this contract filled out."

"Wonderful. Here!" He reached into his shirt pocket and pulled out a pen. "You can use mine."

"Thank you." Maggie accepted the pen and sat on the couch, using the coffee table to write.

Mr. Turner took out his phone and opened his calendar. "I'd recommend it be a two-day sale where we do 30 percent off all prices on the second day. Does that sound good to you?"

"That sounds fine."

"We could prepare everything on July 29 and 30, then hold the sale on July 31 and August 1—that's in two weeks. So, we'd set it all up and price everything on Wednesday and Thursday, and the sale would be on Friday and Saturday. Would those dates work for you?"

"Perfect!" Maggie said as she wrote the dates on the contract and signed her name at the bottom. She stood and handed the papers back to Mr. Turner. "Thank you for getting this done so quickly for me."

"Thank *you* for letting us handle your estate sale, Ms. Maggie."

Chapter 16

"Come on in! Come on in!" Sage opened her front door. "And what do you have there?" she asked as Maggie stepped into the foyer. Maggie was holding a jar in her hands.

"This is for you—fig preserves made from Grandma's figs." She handed Sage the jar.

"Oh! Edith would be so pleased! I am too! I'll eat some of these with biscuits in the morning. Thank you, dear," Sage said as she took the jar with one hand and hugged Maggie with her other. "Now come in here, and let's get comfy. I made us some salad, a shepherd's pie, and an apple pie for dessert."

Maggie sat down at the dining table. "That sounds amazing!"

"Water or tea?" Sage asked as she took her seat.

"Tea, please."

Sage handed Maggie her glass. "So, how did the estate sale meetings go?"

"They went well. The sale will be on July 31 and August 1. I told the man running it that I'd like everything sold except for the piano. I want to keep that."

Sage paused while pouring herself a glass of water and smiled at Maggie. "Oh, I'm so glad you're going to keep Edith's piano. She would be so happy." She finished pouring her drink. "And I'm glad they're getting to you quickly, but I'm gonna be sad when you stop coming around here."

Maggie smiled. "I am too."

"Let me bless it, and we'll get to eating." Sage bowed her head. "Dear Lord, thank You for this food and for our time together. We love You, Father. Amen."

"Amen," Maggie echoed.

"Now help yourself!" Sage scooted the salad bowl closer to Maggie and handed her the tongs.

"I met your grandson today."

Sage nodded as she served herself some of the shepherd's pie. "Yes, that's my youngest grandson—Dylan. He's been mowing for me ever since he got back from college about . . . two years ago."

"So . . . he's like twenty-three?" Maggie asked as she returned the tongs to the salad bowl.

"Turned twenty-four last month."

"Single?" Maggie asked with a grin.

Sage leaned back in her seat and dramatically spread her arms. "No, no, no, Magnolia! You do *not* even want to think about dating Dylan. He's still a man-child. Now I love him—love him more than I can even begin to say—and he's as sweet as can be, but he has a lot of growing up to do. He's *still* hunting for the 'perfect' *job*," Sage said with air quotes. "And while he's out hunting, his mommy and daddy have been paying for everything. He does come here to mow my lawn, and I'm grateful for that. But Dylan doesn't realize that

I know my daughter Penelope—his momma—pays him every week to mow my yard." Sage shrugged. "At least it gets him to stop playing his video games for a bit, and he gets some fresh air."

"I need to pay him for mowing my yard," said Maggie.

"No need, dear. Penelope and her hubby are rolling in the dough. They'll pay him extra for mowing your yard for however long you need it."

Maggie chuckled. "Well, please tell them thank you for me."

"So, I'm guessing from your question about Dylan that you're single. I'd been wondering if you had a special someone."

"No. No, there's no one special. The last guy I seriously dated was about four years ago. He broke up with me a couple of months after Mom and Dad died. He said I was just too much for him to handle, and . . . he said it to me in a text." Maggie had so much more she could say, but she just pursed her lips and looked at Sage.

Sage gasped. "He didn't!"

"Yep—broke up with me in a text."

"Had you two been together long?"

"Almost three years."

"Oh, bless you. That had to be so awful. But I'm thankful you didn't get stuck with him. It's good that he showed you his true, uncompassionate self before you said, 'I do.'"

Sage took a sip of her water. "Find you a man who wants to be a husband—who wants to be a father. Don't pick a man who just wants a wife and children. There's a difference. My Henry wasn't a man-child when I met him. He was already a man. He'd been through Vietnam, and let me tell you, that grew him up quick, bless him. See, he'd been on his own before we met, and I think that's important. Most men need to experience having to do things for themselves before they get married. That way, they're not going from Momma doing everything for them to their wife doing everything for them. That can make a man take his wife for granted. That's why I discouraged you about Dylan. I'm hoping he'll grow up soon, but he's not there yet."

After clearing the dishes from the table, Sage and Maggie took cups of coffee into Sage's living room and sat on the couch together. Maggie noticed her grandmother's book on Egyptian mysteries was sitting on the coffee table.

"I did as you suggested and went over to Edith's to look for keepsakes. I took that book," Sage nodded toward it with her head, "the seashells from the bowl on her piano, and a hot pad she'd knitted. I hope that was okay."

"Absolutely."

"I gave her that book last Christmas. Edith was fascinated with Egypt. She'd checked out every book from the library on pyramids, Egyptian artifacts, mummies—those kinds of things. I think she would've loved to be an archaeologist. Ya know, if that option had ever been available to her."

"Really?"

"Oh, yes."

"Were the seashells from your beach trip together? I saw some photos of you two and another lady at the beach."

Sage threw her head back and laughed. "Oh me . . . I can't even think of that trip without laughing. Our friend, Joyce—she's the one who went with us—she sat down on the porch swing at the house we rented, and when she did, the seat broke, and her bottom hit the porch." Memories sent Sage into a laughing fit. "Her . . . her legs folded up to her face. I mean, she just folded in two. Edith and I tried to help her get back up, but I had just drunk an entire glass of tea, and between laughing and straining to pull Joyce up . . . I totally wet my pants!"

Sage and Maggie both erupted into laughter.

Still giggling, Maggie asked, "What did Grandma do?"

"She wet her skirt!" Sage cackled. "Us old ladies, we have trouble with that sort of thing." Sage wiped her eyes from laughing so hard. "Now . . . now Joyce and I promised Edith we'd never tell anyone about that, but I'm sure you can be trusted." She winked at Maggie. "Oh me, we sure did have the *best* time together." She sighed and then took a sip of her coffee. "I added Edith's shells to my collection," she said, gesturing toward a lamp on the end table closest to Maggie. The glass lamp base was filled with seashells.

Maggie looked around the room and saw a matching shell-filled lamp on the other end table. There was also a glass vase of shells on the fireplace mantel and a bowl of shells on the coffee table.

"I grabbed the hot pad because, years ago, Edith and I were part of a knitting group that used to meet at our church. She and I made matching hot pads, and we joked that they were our 'BFF hot pads.'" Sage glanced down at the mug in her hands. "This may be silly, but it felt weird thinking of some random stranger having the other matching hot pad to mine."

"That's not silly at all," said Maggie. "Could . . . could I have the matching hot pad?" Sage looked up at her as Maggie added, "I'd love to be your new hot pad BFF."

Sage instantly set her cup on the coffee table, hopped up from the couch, and ran to the kitchen. "Of course you can!" She hurried back into the family room and handed the red-and-yellow hot pad to Maggie. "Here you go, BFF!"

Maggie took the knitted square, and Sage gave her a huge hug.

"Will you be here some tomorrow, or do you need to get on back?" Sage asked as she sat back down next to Maggie.

"I was planning on leaving around lunchtime." Maggie rested the hot pad on her knee. "I need to move Grandma's car closer to the road and put a 'For Sale' sign in the window, but that's about all I have planned before I leave. Did you need me?"

"I know this is gonna sound random, but could you please drive me to the library in the morning? It wouldn't take long."

Maggie was a little surprised. Sage seemed to get around fine and obviously had all her senses.

Maybe something's wrong with her car.

"Sure, I can take you."

"Oh, good!"

Maggie asked, "What time do we need to leave?"

"I'll be at your house at nine in the morning, if that's okay?"

"Sounds good."

Chapter 17

"Good morning!"

Maggie turned from locking her front door to see Sage walking over. She had on bright blue capris and a multicolored polka dot blouse. Sage's wardrobe was as vibrant and colorful as her personality.

"Good morning, Sage!" Maggie walked down the front steps and was greeted with a quick hug.

"Let's get this show on the road," Sage said as she marched over to Maggie's car.

As they pulled out of the driveway, Sage continued, "It'll only take about ten minutes to get to the library. You'll just keep going straight until we get to the dollar store, then turn right on the road after it. I don't think I told you this last night—Joyce works at the library. She's been wanting to meet you." Sage giggled and grabbed Maggie's arm. *"Don't* bring up the porch swing incident!"

Maggie laughed. "I won't, I promise."

"There's the dollar store. You'll turn right onto that road. Let me make sure I don't have lipstick on my teeth." Sage pulled the visor down. When she did, a business card fell onto her lap. "Oops!" She picked it up.

"Oh, I forgot I stuck that there," Maggie said as Sage handed her the card.

Maggie set it in the cupholder.

"Barrett Tree Service," Sage said, checking her fuchsia lipstick in the mirror. "Joel Barrett . . ." She closed the visor and turned to look at Maggie. "Now, *he's* a man—not a man-child."

Maggie parked the car and looked at Sage, who was still staring at her, eyebrows raised.

Maggie grinned. "Is he now?"

"Yes, he's an *amazing* young man, and he's single."

"And he lives on his own and takes care of himself?" Maggie asked as they both got out of the car.

"Oh, he's doing more than just taking care of himself," Sage answered while they walked through the parking lot. "Ever since his mom died, he's been helping his dad take care of Owen—his brother. Joel's a fine young man. Yes, he is."

"When did his mom die?"

"About a year ago, from cancer. The whole family took it very hard, especially Owen."

They entered the library through the glass double doors and were greeted by a large circulation desk. Two ladies sat behind the desk; one was Joyce. When she saw them, she clapped her hands, hopped up, and ran around the side of the desk.

"Ohhh! Here y'all are," said Joyce with a thick Southern accent. She grabbed both of Maggie's hands and held them. "I'm Joyce, and I'm so glad to meet you, Magnolia!"

"Thank you!"

Joyce let go of Maggie's hands to quickly hug Sage. "I've been waiting and waiting for y'all to get here!"

"Waiting and waiting?" Sage asked. "The library just opened ten minutes ago!"

"Well, I've been looking forward to this since you called last night, so I've been waiting way longer than ten minutes. Should we go ahead and show her?"

Maggie glanced at Sage's face, then at Joyce's as they stared, grinning back at her. "What are you two up to?"

"Yes." Sage nodded. "Yes, let's show her now."

"Lead the way!" Joyce sang as she locked arms with Maggie.

Sage took off walking with Joyce and Maggie following.

"We have Agatha to thank for this, ya know," Joyce told Maggie, as if Maggie knew who this Agatha person was. "But that's just how she was, always documenting everything. Agatha retired last year—had to after that terrible fall she had. She retired after working here for forty-nine years. It bothered her *so* much that she didn't reach fifty years." Joyce talked a mile a minute as the three ladies walked down aisle after aisle.

Sage stopped at a long cabinet. "Our Library Through the Years" was painted on the wall above the shoulder-high case. It had two long shelves covered with tall, leather-bound books—each with the year printed on the side in gold lettering.

"This was one of Agatha's most prized contributions to the library," Joyce said. "She worked so hard on keeping it up to date. I took over maintaining this section when she left."

Maggie watched as Sage knelt and ran her finger along the books.

"It's in that one—1998," Joyce told her.

Sage pulled the large book from the cabinet. Joyce released Maggie's arm and helped Sage set the book on the nearest table.

"I put a paper in the book to mark the spot," Joyce told Sage as she opened it. "Oh, here it is!"

Maggie couldn't see what they were looking at because the ladies were standing between her and the book. Joyce and Sage turned around, both smiling at her. They stepped back, creating a gap so she could see the book. It was a scrapbook photo album. She slowly moved closer to examine the open pages.

"Calligraphy Fun" was written in calligraphy across the top. Two group photos were pasted below the title. "First Class" was written next to the top picture, and "Last Class" was written next to the bottom photo. Maggie's eyes immediately recognized two people in the top photo.

"Mom," she whispered as her finger gently touched her mom's face. She looked at the young man sitting next to her mother. "Dad," she breathed.

Maggie stood there as her eyes flooded with tears. Sage wrapped an arm around her waist and gave her a squeeze.

Joyce reached into her pocket and pulled out a tissue. "Here, darlin'."

Maggie wiped her eyes and bent down to study the first photo more. She smiled. Her mom and dad looked so young. They were sitting together at a round table. Next to her dad was an elderly lady in a wheelchair.

So, this is my great-grandmother.

She then looked at the girl sitting next to her mom.

And this must be Mom's friend, Sarah.

Maggie looked at the bottom photo. The class was standing in front of a tall bookshelf filled with books. Well, everyone was standing except for her great-grandmother and her dad, who was kneeling beside his grandma's wheelchair. Her mom was standing next to her dad, with Sarah by her side. Each person held a large sheet of paper in front of them. Maggie leaned closer to the book to see the paper in her mom's hands better. It was the same framed Bible verse she'd found hanging in her mother's old bedroom.

"Magnolia, dear?" Sage said. "Joyce is now in charge of this section, and since there are two photos of the group, we thought maybe you'd like to keep the top picture of the day your parents met."

Maggie stood and stared wide-eyed at Joyce. "Could I?"

"Yes, sweetie!" Joyce started peeling the picture from the page. "We want you to have it!"

Chapter 18

"That's amazing!" Hadley said. Maggie had called her while driving back to her apartment. "I mean, how many people actually have a picture of the moment they met their soulmate?"

"Right? Hadley, they look so cute and young! I feel like I'm on the weirdest adventure ever. I thought I knew my parents better than anyone in the world, but I keep finding and learning new things about them."

"I think all parents are different people before they have kids," said Hadley. "So, what's next? Estate sale?"

"Yeah, it's scheduled for the end of the month."

"Do you have to do lots to get it ready, or will the company handle everything?"

"They'll do it all. I may try to get the piano moved out and into my apartment before the sale, but it won't be a

problem if I don't; they'll just put a 'Not for Sale' sign on it."
Maggie glanced at the business card in her cupholder. "And
I think I'm gonna try to move that trunk down from the attic
before the sale. It's heavy, so I'll probably need some help."

"Why not let the estate sale people handle it?"

Maggie paused. "I was thinking I might give that Joel
Barrett a call and ask him to help."

"The good-looking tree guy?"

"Yep."

"This is a good plan. I approve."

After showering and having a late lunch, Maggie got Joel's
business card out of her purse and flopped down on the
couch. She frowned as she studied it. The Barrett Tree Service logo was awful.

His logo is cheesy. He needs my help.

Maggie picked up her phone from the coffee table and
cleared her throat. Settling back into the couch, she dialed
the number on the card.

The phone rang.

No answer.

Joel's voicemail started.

"Hi, you've reached Joel Barrett. Please leave your name
and number, and I'll give you a call back."

"Hi, this is Maggie—Maggie Shaw. We met the other day
at my grandma Edith's house. I was the . . . screaming lady,
but we also met again at the diner, and I was more normal
then. Anyway, you had offered to help me if I needed it, and
I do need some help, so if you could please call me back, that

would be great." Maggie left her number, hung up, closed her eyes, and rested her forehead in her hand.

I am a moron. Definitely should've practiced that first.

As Maggie set her dinner plate in the sink, her phone rang. Sprinting to the living room, she grabbed her phone from the coffee table. It was Hadley.

"Hey," said Maggie.

"You ask tree man to help yet?"

"Sort of—"

"Sort of? How do you *sort of* ask him?"

Maggie's phone beeped to signal an incoming call. She glanced at the screen.

"It's him! He's calling me back! Gotta go!"

Maggie clicked over.

"Hello?" she said calmly.

"Hi, this is Joel Barrett. Is this Maggie?"

"Yeah, it's Maggie. It's—it's me."

"I'm sorry I missed your call earlier, but I got your message. How can I help?"

"Oh, no problem. Thank you for calling me back. I'm having an estate sale at my grandmother's house, and there's a really big, heavy trunk up in the attic. I'd like to bring it down for the sale, but I can't get it down the ladder by myself. Could you—"

"I'd be happy to bring it down for you."

"Oh, good!"

"When would you like me to come over?"

Maggie's toes danced in her slippers. "Could you possibly

meet me there this Saturday afternoon?"

"That should be fine. What time?"

"Two o'clock?"

"Two o'clock—I'll be there."

"Great! Thanks!" Maggie replied. "Umm, well, I won't keep you. I'll see you on Saturday."

"See ya Saturday."

"Bye."

"Bye."

Maggie got into her car after visiting her grandpa. Patricia had noticed she was way more dolled up than her usual Saturday-morning look of exercise clothes and no makeup. After telling Maggie how pretty she looked, Patricia had raised her eyebrows, smiled, and asked, "Meetin' someone *special* later today?" Maggie's grin answered Patricia's question even before she said yes.

Maggie drove the three hours to Jasper. She pulled into the driveway about thirty minutes before Joel would arrive. Before going inside the house, she ran over to Sage's front door and knocked. She'd texted Sage and Hadley after her phone call with Joel, so they both knew about the trunk "date."

Sage opened the door. "Oooo! Now, spin and let me see."

Maggie extended her arms and slowly spun around. She'd curled her hair, spent twice as long on her makeup, and was wearing her curvy jeans, black heels, and a sleeveless, dark purple silk blouse. "Too much? I also brought a fitted green cotton shirt and sandals, too, if you think I should change.”

“Me, oh my! You look absolutely gorgeous!” Sage said. “But here’s a thought: It’s Saturday. What if this trunk-moving soirée goes very well, and he asks you out on a date? Should you wear the green shirt and sandals now and then change into this ensemble for your date?”

“Sage, he’s *not* going to ask me out tonight . . . do you think?”

Sage smiled. “I usually have a good sense about these things, and I think he might—he should, at least, if he has any common sense!”

Maggie took off running back to her car. “Changing!” she sang out as she ran.

Sage laughed and called back, “Good luck!”

Maggie switched her phone to silent. She promised Hadley she’d call right after Joel left, but it would be just like Hadley to call the second he arrived. As she clicked on silent mode, she heard a knock. She walked over to the front door, ran her fingers through her hair, took a deep breath, and exhaled before opening it.

“Hi! Come in, come in!” she said as she moved to the side.

Joel smiled, which showcased his strong jaw and perfect teeth.

Maggie’s heart skipped a beat.

“How are ya doing?” he asked, stepping inside.

“Good. I’m doing good,” Maggie answered as she closed the door. “How are you?”

"I can't complain."

"Thank you so much for helping me with this."

"No problem at all."

Maggie headed up the stairs. "The attic is this way," she said as Joel followed her.

When she reached the attic's rope, Joel stepped around her and said, "Let me get that for you." He pulled the door open and lowered the ladder.

"Thank you."

Maggie climbed into the attic, pulled out her phone, and turned on the flashlight. After Joel had made his way up, she motioned to the old trunk and said, "Here it is. It's empty but still pretty heavy."

Joel walked over and, with no effort, picked it up. The muscles in his arms strained against his T-shirt's sleeves. He carried the trunk back over to the attic door and set it down.

"Let me run out to my truck real quick and get a rope. I think the best way to get it down the ladder is for me to lower it. I'll be right back."

After he climbed down, Maggie texted Hadley:

> Okay, he picked up the trunk like it was a feather! His arms are HUGE!

Hadley texted back:

> I love muscley men!!! 🖤

After a couple of minutes, Joel climbed back up the ladder, carrying a rope. He tied it to the handle on one end of the trunk.

"Just let me know if I can help," said Maggie.

"Thanks, but this should be easy."

Maggie happily watched as he lowered the trunk through

the attic's opening.

"Let me go and move it out of the way before you climb down," Joel said, descending the ladder.

Maggie waited a few seconds before he called up, "Okay, you're good now."

When she stepped off the ladder, Joel pushed it up and closed the attic door.

"Where would you like me to set it?" he asked, untying the rope.

"In this room." Maggie motioned to her mom's old bedroom. "You can just put it at the end of the bed."

Joel picked up the trunk, carried it to the foot of the twin bed, and set it down. He then walked back to the hall where Maggie was waiting.

"Need any help with anything else?" he asked as he coiled the rope back up.

I wish. Think of something else he can do!

"No, I think that was it. Thank you. I don't know how I would've gotten that trunk in here by myself."

Maggie led the way back down the stairs, with Joel following her.

"Have you got a busy weekend planned?" he asked. "You and Sage hitting the town tonight? She taking you dancing?"

Maggie laughed.

"You know Sage is big into line dancing, right?" said Joel.

Maggie spun around and looked at him as she reached the foyer. "Is she really?"

"Oh, yes. She and a few ladies from church are in a line dancing class at the senior center."

"Why does that *not* surprise me?" Maggie chuckled. "I just love her."

Joel stood by the door. "So . . . no line dancing plans for you tonight?" His eyes locked onto Maggie's as he asked.

"No," Maggie answered. "I don't have any plans tonight."

"As it turns out, I don't have any plans tonight either.

Could I—" He looked down for a second, then back at Maggie. "Could I take you to dinner?"

"Yes."

Chapter 19

"I knew it! I just knew it!" Sage shouted over the phone.

Maggie laughed. "I'm so glad you encouraged me to save my dressier outfit."

"So, where's he taking you?"

"I'm not sure. He's picking me up at six."

"This is so exciting! Promise you'll let me know how it all goes?"

"Yes, ma'am. I promise."

"Okay, dear. I'll talk to you later."

"Bye."

"Bye-bye."

Maggie hung up and called Hadley, filling her in on the news too.

Right at six o'clock, Joel knocked on the door. Maggie answered to find he'd also changed clothes. He was now wearing a dark blue button-up with the sleeves rolled just below his elbows and nicer jeans. This was the first time she'd seen him without a ball cap. His light brown hair was short and perfectly disheveled.

He smiled at her. "You look beautiful."

The immediate compliment caught Maggie off guard. "Oh . . . thank you."

"Ready to go?"

She reached for her purse on the coffee table. "Ready."

"Okay, there are two options I was thinking of for dinner," Joel said as they headed to his truck. "One's an Italian restaurant, and the other's a steak house." He opened the passenger side door for Maggie.

"Umm, Italian sounds great," she said, climbing in.

"Italian, it is," he replied with a nod and then closed her door.

As Joel walked around to his side of the truck, Maggie glanced toward Sage's house and saw Sage in the side window, giving her a thumbs-up. She laughed and gave her a quick wave.

"Owen will be thrilled that you picked the Italian place." Joel shut his door and started the truck. "He loves their breadsticks and asked me to bring him home some if we ate there."

"Good! Then I picked right."

Joel smiled. "Whatever you'd have picked would've been right."

Maggie and Joel were sitting next to a window at a table for two. The restaurant was dimly lit with a candle-like lamp on each table, and soft music played in the background. The waiter brought their plates to the table. Joel had ordered lasagna, and Maggie got chicken parmigiana.

"This looks good. I'll bless it." Joel extended his hand to Maggie, who placed her hand in his.

Maggie's heart beat faster.

He may be perfect.

"Dear Lord," Joel prayed, "thank You for this meal and for this time with Maggie. Amen."

"Amen," Maggie echoed.

As they ate, they talked about some usual first date topics. Maggie learned that Joel was twenty-five, had lived in Jasper his whole life, and was a huge Arkansas Razorbacks fan.

They then discussed their jobs. Maggie shared first and then said, "Okay, your turn—tell me all about your job."

"My dad and his two brothers started Barrett Tree Service before I was born. My uncle Dave, his older brother, moved away when I was a senior in high school, and that's when I began helping Dad. Once I graduated, I joined the team full-time. Then my cousin, Kyle, and my brother, Owen—who you've already met—both joined us a couple years after that."

Joel took a drink.

"When Owen started working with us, my mom was really worried about him 'cause he doesn't react quickly to unexpected things, ya know—if something were to go wrong. And he struggled with the loud sounds at first, but Dad found the perfect job for him. Owen waits in my truck until we get everything cut into logs, and then he stacks all the lumber. Owen's really strong, and he's a hard worker."

"It must be nice working with your family, seeing them all the time," said Maggie.

"It is. I've heard some people say that working with family is rough, but it's a good fit for me. Do you have a large family?" Joel asked.

"No, I'm an only child, so it was just my mom, dad, and me. We were super close with my dad's parents. My dad was also an only child, and so was my mom. So, no aunts or uncles, no cousins or anything like that. My dad's mom— my grandma Jane—died six years ago, and my mom and dad passed away four years ago in a car accident." Saying that last sentence made Maggie's throat tighten a bit. She swallowed. "So now it's only my grandpa and me."

"I'm so sorry. If you don't want to talk about that, we don't have to."

"I don't mind talking about them. It was hard for the first couple of years, and it still is sometimes, but it also feels good to talk about them. There's lots of great memories and stories that are fun to share."

Joel stared at the table and nodded. He took another drink.

Looking back at her, he said, "My mom died almost a year ago. It feels . . . good to hear that you do get to a place where you can talk about them again without . . . falling apart." He gave an embarrassed smile while tears formed in his eyes.

Maggie reached across the table and patted his hand.

Joel blinked a few times and looked to the side.

"We don't have to talk about families anymore," Maggie offered.

"No, no. I don't mind." He sniffed and looked at Maggie

again. "For some reason, I want to talk about her with you."

His eyes drifted down the table while he thought for a moment. "My mom was an amazing woman. I miss her. And I—I worry about Owen. Dad and I were really close to Mom, but Owen . . . she was his whole world. She thought it would be best for Owen if she homeschooled him, so they spent every single day together. After that, the only time he wasn't with Mom was when he was at work with us, but honestly, most days, she'd come and sit in the truck with Owen until we'd finished the felling. They were attached at the hip. He hasn't been the same since she left. It's like . . . his light—his spark—is gone. She knew how to push and encourage him. Dad and I try, but we're not as good at it as she was."

He smiled at Maggie. "I love my brother. He's five years younger than me, and he's amazing. I just . . . I miss how happy he used to be." Tears returned to his eyes. "Good grief." He looked to the side and chuckled. "I'm sorry you're on a date with such a crybaby."

"No, no—don't apologize. We belong to a club that many people can't relate to. But I understand. And I've found that time doesn't heal the pain, but it does make us stronger so we can make it through."

Joel stared at her. Normally, this amount of unwavering eye contact would make Maggie squirm and feel uncomfortable. But it didn't.

"Could I please see you again?" Joel finally asked, his eyes so intense.

"Yes," was all she could manage to say.

Chapter 20

Joel and Maggie talked on the phone every night until Saturday. They discussed books, food, music, their faith, favorite vacation spots, hobbies, family memories, sports, hopes, and dreams—they talked for hours every evening.

Maggie visited her grandpa on Saturday morning and then drove to Jasper for her second date with Joel. He picked her up at six and took her to a local pizza place.

She set her purse on the table and was about to slide into the booth when Joel stopped her by saying, "Hey, would you mind if I sit on that side and you sit here?" He motioned to the seat opposite her.

"Sure," Maggie answered, picking up her purse.

That's weird.

As Maggie sat on the other side, she looked up to see a wall of TVs in front of her—all showing football games.

"Thanks, I didn't want to be distracted," Joel said, sliding into his seat. He smiled at her. "I came here to be with you, not watch football."

Okay. He's perfect.

After ordering, Joel said, "So, the estate sale's coming up. Need any help getting things ready for it?"

"No, the company's handling everything, but thanks. Sage is going to let them use her key when they come to prep for the sale and during it. I'll come in on Saturday when it's winding down so I can see how it went and get the check from them."

Joel grinned. "Could I please take you out next Saturday night?"

Maggie smiled and nodded. "You'll get to see me again before Saturday, though."

"How's that?"

"Sage invited me to go to church with her in the morning."

"She did? Great!"

"And she told me something I didn't know."

"What's that?"

"You play guitar in the church band."

"I do," Joel said as he moved his drink aside so the waiter could place their pizza on the table.

"So I'll get to hear you play tomorrow. I'm excited!"

"And now I'm nervous."

Maggie laughed. "You'll do great."

After church, Maggie ate lunch at Sage's house before heading back to her apartment. On the drive, she called Hadley.

"You didn't text me back after your date!" said Hadley. "So, did Mr. Lumberjack kiss you last night?"

"Nope."

"He's a slow-mover."

"He is not, and he gave me a great hug."

"Oh, goody! Maybe next time he'll give you a high five! You know I don't go for kissing after a first date, but after a second date . . ."

"We don't all move as quickly as you do, my dear."

Hadley gasped playfully. "Okay, shade thrower!"

"Besides, waiting will just make it more special when he does finally kiss me. Oh, guess what! He plays the guitar and, like, really well!"

Hadley sighed. "That's so hot. Ever notice that guys who are only a little cute turn way cuter when they play an instrument?"

"Absolutely, but he's already gorgeous, so now he's . . . I don't even have a word to describe how good-looking he is now."

"Do I get to be in your wedding?"

Maggie laughed. "It's only been two weeks! Little early to be planning a wedding."

"Just wait—I can tell. He's the one."

The week flew by quickly. Maggie visited her grandpa on Tuesday after work. He didn't remember her, but he was in a good mood. On Wednesday evening, Hadley and Maggie went to see a movie together. Mr. Turner informed her on Thursday that everything was good to go for the estate sale, and on

Friday evening, he called to tell her that the first day had gone great.

Maggie had talked to Joel every night before bed. She loved his sense of humor, his thoughtfulness, how he not only listened to her but also remembered what she said, his calm energy, his hardworking nature, and his closeness to his family. After each phone call, Maggie found herself agreeing with Hadley more and more; Joel really was "the one."

On Saturday morning, Maggie visited her grandpa again. Patricia met her in the hallway. "Ms. Maggie, Mr. Liam is havin' a hard day. He had a difficult time in the bathroom this mornin' and has been very agitated and upset ever since. And after breakfast, he started tellin' me over and over that he doesn't know where it is."

"Where what is?" Maggie asked.

Patricia shrugged. "There's just no tellin'. I've tried handin' him some things, but he just throws 'em."

"Throws them?" Maggie repeated, wide-eyed.

"Not *at* me. He throws them down on the ground. He's not bein' physically aggressive, but I do want you to be cautious when you're near him."

Maggie stared at her grandpa's door, her brow furrowed.

"This is somethin' we warn all families about when their loved ones reach this stage. You and I both know your grandpa would never harm a fly when he's in his right mind, but dementia sometimes flips an aggressive switch. So you be careful, okay?"

Maggie didn't know what to say. She'd never even considered that her grandpa could ever physically hurt her.

Noticing her hesitation, Patricia asked, "You want me to sit and visit with you two?"

"Would you mind?"

"I don't mind at all! Let's go," Patricia said as she walked with Maggie to her grandpa's room.

He didn't act out, but he barely spoke either. His face

looked so distressed, and he kept muttering to himself. Maggie's heart broke as she watched him repeatedly try to unbutton and then button his shirt.

Maggie usually stayed about an hour, but she cut this visit short. She felt overwhelmed and alone. Without thinking, she grabbed her phone the second she got in her car and called Joel.

"Hey!"

Maggie tried to speak, but she began to cry.

"Maggie? What's wrong? Are you okay?"

She took a breath and explained what had happened.

"I'm so sorry."

"I . . . I just feel alone and scared. I wish I had my family here to help me know how to take care of him."

"If there's anything I can do, please tell me. I'll do anything to help you."

Maggie smiled. "Thank you. Talking to you helps. I want to see you tonight, but I don't know how fun of a date I'll be. I really don't feel like being with a lot of people."

"Let's stay at your grandma's house then."

"There's no furniture there now."

"Leave it all to me. I'll take care of it."

The estate sale was a success. When Maggie arrived at the house, there were only a couple of pieces of furniture and a few little trinkets remaining.

Mr. Turner, the estate sale liquidator, walked over to her. "Ms. Maggie, let me introduce you to Mr. Jones," he said, motioning to a short man with quite an impressive comb-over. "He comes to the end of estate sales and sees if he can purchase everything that's left for a price."

Mr. Jones made Maggie an offer, which she accepted.

After Mr. Turner handed Maggie a check and Sage's key, he and his team left. Maggie stood in her grandmother's family room, empty except for the piano. Despite the sale's success, the house looked sad—like Maggie felt.

She slowly approached and removed the "Not for Sale" sign from the piano.

There was a knock at the door. Maggie opened it, expecting to see Sage, but it was Joel.

She smiled. "You're here early." As he hugged her, she added, "I didn't expect you for another couple of hours."

"I was waiting in the driveway for everyone to leave. I didn't want to be in the way." He glanced around. "Looks like the sale was a success."

"It was."

"Okay, I need you to wait here. I'll be right back."

Joel stepped outside, leaving the door slightly ajar. A minute later, he returned, pushing the door open with his foot. He came inside, carrying a basket of food, a cooler, a bouquet of flowers, and a blanket.

"How about a picnic in the living room?"

Maggie tried to smile, but crying overtook her.

"Hey, come here. Come here," Joel said as he set everything but the flowers down. He wrapped his arm around her and pulled her close.

"Thank you," she whispered.

"You're welcome." He stepped back and looked at her. "These are for you," he said, handing her the flowers.

Maggie smiled as she wiped the tears from her cheeks. "They're beautiful, but I—I don't have a vase to put them in."

"Hold on!" Joel ran out the front door again, this time returning with a vase and a box.

Maggie laughed. "You thought of everything!"

"Tried to," he said, setting the box down on the floor. He handed the vase to Maggie. "Will you please fill this with water while I get our picnic set up here?"

Maggie carried the flowers and vase into the kitchen, while Joel spread out the blanket and set out the food.

"Owen helped me make us some sandwiches, pasta salad, and cookies," he called out. "I also have some chips and pickles."

"Sounds perfect," Maggie said as she returned, setting the vase of flowers on the piano. She sat down on the blanket next to Joel, and he handed her a paper plate.

He motioned to the plastic food containers. "Help yourself."

They ate, talked, and laughed. Maggie hadn't been cared for like this in years.

When they finished eating, Joel pulled a trash bag out of the basket.

"You really did think of everything," Maggie said in astonishment. "I've never met a man like you before—I mean that in a good way."

Joel smiled with pride as he cleaned up. When he finished, he placed the bag next to the front door and picked up the box.

"Okay, I have something to give you."

Chapter 21

"Something else for me?" Maggie asked.

"Yes." Joel sat back down next to her and placed the box between them. He looked nervous. "I've had this for a couple of weeks. I was holding onto it because I wanted to wait to give it to you." He looked her in the eyes. "I didn't . . . I didn't want to come on too strong too quickly." He took a deep breath and exhaled. "But you've had a hard day, and I think—I *hope* this gift is a nice surprise and makes you happy."

He picked up the box and handed it to her.

Maggie had no idea what could be inside.

She looked at Joel and smiled. "I'm a bit nervous now to open it."

"You and me both."

Maggie glanced down at the box in her hands. A small

piece of tape sealed the flaps shut. She peeled it back and opened the box.

Inside was a large bowl—a large *wooden* bowl.

She lifted it out of the box, set it on her lap, and looked at Joel.

"That day . . . when we cut down your grandmother's magnolia tree, I took some of the best logs."

Maggie stared at him.

"See, I have a friend who's a woodturner, and I took the logs to him and asked him to make you something."

Maggie didn't move or speak.

"I—I just saw how upset you were to lose that tree, and I thought you might like having a keepsake from it so you could—"

"I love you."

Maggie was just as shocked when the words left her mouth as Joel was to hear them. They both stared wide-eyed at each other.

WHAT DID I JUST SAY? He's not even kissed me yet! What do I do? What do I do? What do I—?

Joel interrupted her racing thoughts by gently placing his hand on her cheek and kissing her. He pulled his face a few inches away from hers and looked into her eyes.

"I love you too," he whispered.

He closed his eyes and rested his forehead against Maggie's. She shut her eyes too. They sat in silence, breathing in the moment.

After a minute, Joel kissed her again. As they kissed, she rested her hand on his chest and felt his heart pounding—just like hers.

Joel settled back into his spot on the blanket.

"I'm so sorry I said that," Maggie confessed, looking down at the bowl in her lap. The feelings of embarrassment and vulnerability kept her from looking at him. "I mean, I'm not sorry that I feel that way. I'm just sorry I said it so soon in our relationship. Was it—" She peered up at him. "Is it too soon?"

"You definitely surprised me. And if anyone else had told me they loved me after three weeks of dating, I'd have freaked out." He smiled and reached for her hand. "But I'm not. I fell for you on our first date."

"You did?"

He nodded. "But I kinda wish I hadn't kissed you yet."

"What?" Maggie sat up straight. "Why?"

"Because now it's all I want to do."

Maggie smiled as he leaned forward and kissed her again.

He's a great kisser!

She picked up the wooden bowl. "This is amazing," she said, examining it more. "My mom used to play in that magnolia tree. She loved it," she explained, still studying the bowl. "It's why she named me Magnolia."

"I'm so sorry we cut it down."

Maggie set the bowl back on her lap. "No, no. You gave her tree back to me." She put her hand on his. "Thank you."

"You're welcome."

"And thank you for the picnic and for the flowers," Maggie said as she looked at the vase on the piano.

"Will you play something for me?" Joel asked, following her gaze.

She looked back at him. He knew she could play the piano because they had discussed it one night on the phone when she'd explained to him why she was keeping the piano— because her grandma had taught her mom how to play on it— but Maggie had never played in front of anyone except her parents and grandparents. And that had been years ago. Her nerves would have told anyone else no, but for some reason, Joel didn't make her feel nervous about playing.

"Sure," she said softly. She set the bowl on the floor beside her, stood up, and went to the piano. "Any requests?"

"Anything you'd like to play."

Maggie rested her fingers on the keys while she thought. She started playing "River Flows in You."

Joel sat and listened, mesmerized by the music—but mostly by Maggie.

"You said what?" Hadley shouted into the phone.

Joel had just left, and Maggie was too excited to wait another minute to fill Hadley in. She knew Sage went to bed around nine, so she'd call her in the morning to give her the news.

"And you said *I'm* the quick mover?" Hadley teased.

"I know! I know. It just slipped out because . . . I *do* love him. I've never felt this way before."

"I probably would've said the same thing if he'd given me a gift like that. I mean, Maggie, he saved that wood and took it to his friend and paid for the bowl—all for you—before he'd even asked you out on a date!"

"I know," Maggie said, gazing at her vase of flowers.

"And just think! Every time you look at that bowl, you'll not only think of your mom, but you'll remember your and Joel's first kiss! This is so romantic." Hadley sighed. "I need a man. Want to introduce me to the neighbor's shirtless grandson?"

Maggie laughed. "I do want you to come with me sometime to meet Joel and Sage. Hadley, it feels—it feels magical here." She was sitting on the piano bench, looking around the empty room. "I'm going to miss this place."

After getting off the phone, Maggie went to her car and

grabbed her air mattress, sleeping bag, pillow, and overnight bag. She'd only used the sleeping bag and air mattress once before, when Hadley had invited her to go camping. Hadley's family—her entire extended family—went on a weekend-long camping trip every fall. They'd done this for over twenty years.

After Maggie's parents died, Hadley invited her to go on the camping trip. Maggie almost didn't go; she worried that watching Hadley with her family would be too much for her to handle. But at the last minute, she decided to tag along, and she was so glad she did. A weekend in a tent with Hadley and four of her girl cousins was exactly what Maggie needed. She'd laughed again for the first time in months.

That trip was the only time she'd used the sleeping bag and air mattress, so she'd almost donated them last year but was now thankful she hadn't.

She made herself a bed on the living room floor, went upstairs to the bathroom, and got ready for bed.

Chapter 22

The next morning, Maggie walked over to Sage's house. It was humid, and the freshly cut grass was wet, sticking to her toes and heels. Sage had invited Maggie to church again. Maggie brought the bowl to show Sage before they left. She stomped her feet on the steps to try to lose some of the wet grass. She hid the bowl behind her back and rang the doorbell.

Sage opened her front door. "Good morning, Mag—what do you have there?"

Maggie was beaming. "A gift that Joel gave me last night." She brought the wooden bowl out from behind her back and held it up for Sage to see.

"Oh, how beautiful," Sage said as she stepped onto the porch, touching the smooth bowl.

"Sage, it's made with the wood from Mom's tree."

Sage gasped and covered her mouth with her hand. As

she stared down at the bowl, she slowly placed both of her hands on Maggie's arms. "Oh, Magnolia. This is special . . . very special." She looked at Maggie. "*Joel* is special! He's a keeper, darling!"

"I know! I've never had any man treat me the way he does."

"He does it because he loves you, dear," Sage said matter-of-factly as she locked her door. Taking hold of Maggie's arm, they walked down the porch steps together.

"I love him too," Maggie said softly.

"Isn't it the best feeling in the world?"

"It is."

Maggie stopped walking when they got back over to her house.

"Let me put the bowl back in the house real quick," she told Sage. "The car's unlocked, so you can go ahead and get in."

On the drive to church, Sage asked about the estate sale.

"It went great! I have your key in my purse," Maggie answered. "I'll give it back to you when we get there."

"Had any inquiries on Edith's car yet?"

"One, but it fell through. What I need to do next is find a realtor and get the house listed."

"Would you want to talk to Tony Baker?" Sage asked as she pulled down the visor mirror and checked to make sure her red lipstick wasn't on her teeth. "He's a real estate agent who goes to my church."

"That would be great!"

After the church service, Maggie used the three-hour drive home to make some phone calls. First, she called the memory care facility and spoke to Patricia. She wanted to see how her grandpa was doing. The update wasn't what she'd hoped for; he was still out of sorts and agitated.

Next, she called Joel.

After their hellos, Joel said, "You looked amazing today—as always."

Maggie grinned. "Thank you. You played amazing today."

"Why, thank you, ma'am."

"You're welcome." Maggie's expression and voice dropped. "Well, I have some bad news and some good news. Bad news is that my grandpa isn't doing any better today."

"I'm sorry."

"I'm worried that his good days or good moments are disappearing completely."

"I'm praying for him."

"Thank you." Maggie let out a small sigh as her brain shifted gears. "The good news is that Sage introduced me to Tony Baker, and I think he's gonna take care of selling the house. He's going to meet me there on Friday to walk through it."

"Tony's a good man."

"That's what Sage said."

"So you'll need to leave work early on Friday?"

"Yeah, I'll leave at lunch because I have to meet him at three-thirty."

"Your boss okay with all this still?"

"Oh yeah, she's being so understanding. As long as I turn in my work on time, she's good with it. I told her that once the house and car sell, I won't have to keep driving to Jasper."

Silence.

"But I'll still come on weekends to see you," Maggie assured him. "I just mean I won't miss work to drive there."

"And I'll drive to you too."

"Ooo, speaking of that, could you possibly help me get the piano to my apartment sometime?"

"Absolutely. Okay if I ask Owen to help?"

"Sure!"

"Now I have a question for you."

"Okay, ask away."

"After you meet with Tony on Friday, could you come over to my house for dinner? I know you've met my dad at church and all, but I'd like for him and Owen to get to know you."

Maggie smiled. "I'd love that."

"Good, good."

Maggie could tell from his voice that Joel was smiling too. Then she heard him start to say something, but he hesitated.

"When you come over," he started, "Owen will . . . well, I just want to give you a heads-up about him. He was diagnosed with autism when he was four years old. I was nine, and my mom explained one of the things Owen deals with to me like this. She said that he has 'Think It – Say It.' So, anything that Owen thinks will come straight out of his mouth. He has no filter. He's gotten better about it as he's gotten older, but most of the time, he'll still tell you exactly what he thinks."

"That's okay."

"Honestly, I usually enjoy that about him. It's refreshing to know that when he says something nice, you know he really means it. And when he flaps his hands, you know that he's truly happy. He's not trying to hide it. Like, there's no mental games or hinting at stuff. He's just . . . honest."

"Joel, I'm excited about coming over and having dinner with your family. It's gonna be great."

"Thank you."

Maggie heard him let out a deep breath.

"Oh! And I have another question to ask you!" he said. "Sorry to bombard you with invites, but my cousin, Kyle, is getting married in . . . I think it's three weeks. I'll check on that and make sure I tell you the right date. Would you go with me?"

Maggie beamed. "Yes, I will."

"Now, I won't get to sit with you during the ceremony 'cause Owen and I are groomsmen, but they're not doing a wedding party table at the reception. So, we can be together then. Would that be okay?"

"That'll be fine. Is it black-tie or . . . how should I dress?"

"Uhhh . . . I'll send you a picture of their invitation to make sure I don't tell you wrong."

Maggie chuckled. "Good idea."

Joel paused. "Maggie, if I'm overwhelming you with all these invites, just let me know."

"You're not. I *want* to be with you."

"I want to be with you too . . . all the time."

Maggie's heart danced in her chest.

Chapter 23

On Friday, Maggie went to work and then, as planned, left at lunch. She drove to Jasper and met Tony at the house. He took lots of interior and exterior photos to list on his company's website.

When Tony left, Maggie got her overnight bag and pillow from her car and walked over to Sage's house. Sage hadn't been happy when she found out that Maggie had slept on the floor the previous weekend and insisted that from now on, Maggie stay in her guestroom anytime she was in town.

Sage opened the front door. "Come in, come in! This is going to be so fun having you stay the night! I've been excited about it all week!"

"I'm excited too!" Maggie said as she closed the front door. "I wish I could stay the weekend and not have to leave so early tomorrow." She'd already let Sage know that she needed to leave by seven so she could visit her grandpa.

"Your grandpa is blessed to have you, Magnolia." Sage turned and headed down the hall. "This way!" she said, motioning for Maggie to follow.

"Here's your room," Sage said, flicking on the lights to the room just past the bathroom. The guest room smelled of lemons and was, of course, decorated with beach colors and décor.

Maggie set her pillow on the bed and her bag on the floor. "Thank you. This is perfect."

"Well, I don't know about perfect, but it'll be much comfier than Edith's floor! Now, what time do you need to leave to go to Joel's?"

"He said it'll take about twenty minutes to get to his house, so I'll leave here around five-thirty."

Maggie unzipped her bag and pulled out a red short-sleeved blouse.

"I was thinking of leaving on these jeans and changing into this top," Maggie said, holding up the blouse. "What do you think?"

"Ooo, yes. And I'd wear some nice red lipstick with it."

Maggie smiled. "I don't usually wear much lipstick. Do you think it would look good on me?"

"Oh, yes. Honey, lipstick and earrings are the keys to looking put-together."

When Maggie was ready to leave, Sage was thrilled to see that she had followed her advice. She was wearing red lipstick and small silver hoop earrings.

Maggie got in her car and headed toward Joel's address. She'd driven about five minutes when her phone rang. It was Joel.

"I'm sorry I'm only now getting a chance to call," he said. "The truck had a flat, and we were parked in a muddy field. I'm filthy and running late."

"Oh, I'm sorry."

"Where are you now?"

Maggie looked around. "I'm about to pass the dollar store."

"Okay, I should get to my house before you. I'll jump in the shower as fast as I can and get cleaned up. Dad and Owen are there, so they'll let you in."

"That's fine. I'll see you in a bit."

"Love you."

Maggie grinned. They'd said those words to each other after every phone call since he'd given her the bowl, but hearing him say it still made her heart flutter.

"Love you too."

Maggie pulled into the driveway of a two-story brick house. She parked and, like Sage, checked her red lipstick in the visor mirror to make sure it wasn't on her teeth. She got out, walked to the front door, and rang the doorbell.

Owen opened the door.

He stared down to his side, but said, "Come in."

"Hi, Owen!" Maggie said as she walked into the foyer.

Owen glanced at her face for a couple of seconds. When he did, he frowned and grunted before looking away again.

"Your lips are red," he said.

"Yes, I'm wearing red lipstick. Does it look okay?"

"No. You look like a clown," he said in a straight tone.

She smiled. "Sage told me she thought it would look nice. Do you think Joel will like the way it looks?"

"No. I think he'd like your mouth to look normal."

Her smile widened. "Well, let's see." She opened her purse and pulled out her compact. "Owen, could you please get me a paper towel?"

Without answering, Owen left her in the foyer for a minute. He returned and handed her a paper towel.

"Thank you," she said, taking the towel from him.

Maggie looked into her compact mirror and wiped off the red lipstick. When she finished, her lips still had a tint of the color, but it was much more muted.

"Does this look better?" she asked.

Owen glanced quickly at her face.

"Yes."

Maggie crumpled the paper towel and put it, along with her compact, into her purse.

"Thank you for helping me, Owen."

"My mom always said I was a great helper," Owen said, still staring down to the side.

Ray, Joel's dad, joined them in the foyer.

"Maggie! Welcome! Come on in," he said, gesturing for her to step into the family room. "Joel should be down any second. I was on the back porch, finishing up the grilling. We're having salad, steak, and potatoes. That sound okay?"

"Sounds wonderful," Maggie answered.

"I'm having chicken fingers and tater tots," Owen said.

"Yeah, Owen isn't a fan of steaks and baked potatoes," Ray explained. "The textures don't sit well with him. Speaking of sitting, have a seat." He motioned to the couch.

After Maggie sat down, Ray took the leather chair, and Owen settled into a wooden rocker. The room had a farmhouse shabby chic vibe.

"Your home is lovely," said Maggie.

"Well, thank you," Ray said as he looked around the room. "We can't take any credit for the decorating—that was all Jenny."

Maggie saw Owen's back stiffen.

"She loved her some chickens," Ray said.

Maggie glanced around the family room and saw what he was talking about. There were little porcelain chickens on the shelves, a framed chicken picture, and a cushion on the couch with an embroidered chicken on it.

"Do you all have chickens?" Maggie asked.

"We do—got eight in the backyard," Ray answered. "If you ever want any fresh eggs, you just let us know."

"Thank you."

Joel walked down the stairs into the family room. His hair was wet, and he was smiling at Maggie. Her breath caught in her throat the moment she saw him.

"Sorry you all had to wait on me," he said, walking over to sit next to her.

"Worth the wait 'cause you smell a lot better than you did when you got home," Ray said with a playful smile.

"Unfortunately, I think a lot of that mud was manure," Joel said, settling next to Maggie. "But I'm clean now," he told her. "You find the house okay?"

"Yep, not a bad drive at all."

Ray smacked his knees. "Well," he said as he stood up, "let's eat!"

"So, Joel tells me you're a graphic designer," Ray said as he cut into his steak.

Maggie wiped her mouth with her napkin. "Yes, I mainly design business logos and social media ads."

"Joel said that maybe we should have you make us a logo," Ray said. "The one we have on the truck and our business cards was made by my brother years ago. Joel thinks we need to update it."

Yes, please. Let me help you.

Maggie smiled at Joel, then glanced back at Ray. "I'd be happy to design you all some options to look at."

"All right, then," said Ray. "That's settled."

Joel smiled and nodded at Maggie.

"But there's still something else that needs settling," Ray said as he put butter on his potato. "Do we post about the job or wait a bit longer to decide?"

"I really think we need to go ahead and hire someone," Joel answered.

"What do you think, Owen?" Ray asked.

"Okay," Owen responded, staring at his plate.

"Mom always handled the bookkeeping for the business," Joel explained to Maggie. "Invoices, bookings, payroll, schedules, taxes . . . all of it."

"Yep," Ray said. "And we've learned that we always had the easier part of the job compared to all that she did."

"Dad and I have been trying to handle all the bookkeeping while still doing the physical labor, and we just can't do it all," Joel said. "We need to hire someone."

"And soon," Ray added. Reaching for his drink, he noticed that Owen had stopped eating and was rocking back and forth in his seat. Ray glanced at Joel before saying, "Maybe after we eat, Owen could show Maggie his marble tower. He got it for his birthday, and it sure is something else."

Owen didn't say anything or move.

"I'd like that," said Maggie. "Owen, would you please

show it to me?"

Owen set his napkin on the table and started to stand.

"Let's show her after we all finish eating," said Joel.

Owen settled back into his chair and picked up a chicken finger.

After the meal, Maggie began clearing the table, but Ray insisted that he and Owen had it covered, and that Maggie and Joel go into the family room.

When Joel and Maggie sat on the couch, she reached for her purse and pulled out a small notebook and pen.

"Okay, tell me some ideas you have for the new logo."

She jotted down Joel's thoughts and started sketching some ideas out. As she drew, Owen quietly came up beside her and watched.

Maggie jumped when he emphatically said, "That line shouldn't go there."

She looked up at him. "Which line?"

Owen pointed to a line at the bottom of the design. "That line should be on the side," he stated.

"Will you show me where?" Maggie asked.

She watched as Owen pointed to the left side of the sketch.

Maggie erased the line she'd drawn at the bottom and moved it to where Owen had directed her.

"Like this?" she asked.

"Yes." Owen walked over, sat in the wooden rocker, and started rocking.

Maggie studied the sketch. The moved line did make the design look more cohesive.

She smiled. "Owen, you have a great eye for design."

"He's a great helper," said Joel.

"Mom always said I was a great helper," Owen said as he rocked. Even with his face angled downward, she could see that he looked sad.

Maggie glanced at Joel.

"Hey, Owen?" Maggie said as she put the notebook and pencil back into her purse. "Could you please show me your marble tower now?"

Owen stood up and headed upstairs. Joel and Maggie followed him to his bedroom. Maggie watched as he picked up a few marbles from a small bowl on his dresser. Owen sat on the floor beside a plastic tower of curving tracks and tunnels. As the marbles zoomed through the tower, Owen rocked, flapped his hands, and smiled.

Chapter 24

The next morning, Maggie drove the three hours to visit her grandpa. Liam was in a calmer mood, but he didn't make much sense when he spoke. Maggie worried that he'd become flustered from not being able to find his words, so she played some of his favorite music on her phone. He tapped his fingers, nodded his head, and occasionally hummed along. They sat together for almost an hour, just listening to the music and watching the tree outside his window.

As Maggie left the memory care facility, she called Joel.

"Hey!" she said as she got into her car.

"Hey, babe."

"I'm just leaving from seeing Grandpa."

"How was he today?"

"Better. He struggled to find words, so we just listened to music together. But he was in a much better mood than he has been, so that was good."

"Good. I'm glad."

"What are you up to?" Maggie asked as she pulled out of her parking place.

"Dad and I were going over this week's schedule, and listen, we don't have anything on the calendar for this Tuesday. Would you want Owen and me to load the piano and bring it to you that day? Dad has a trailer we can use to haul it."

"That would be great! You can use Sage's key to get into the house."

"Sounds good."

"I'll call Sage in a bit and let her know." Maggie paused. "Hey . . . could you possibly come visit my grandpa with me on Tuesday? I usually go by to see him after work. I know it could be awkward because he's struggling, but . . . I'd really like for you to meet him . . . while you can."

"I'd love to meet him. Is it okay that Owen will be with me?"

"Will Owen mind?"

"No, as long as I'm with him, he should be fine with stopping by."

"Thank you," said Maggie.

"You're welcome. You get off at five on Tuesday, right?"

"Yeah."

"Would you be okay with us stopping by your office to get your apartment key? Then we could take the piano to your place, unload it, and be back at your office in time to follow you to your grandpa's when you get off. That sound okay?"

"Perfect. And can I please take you and Owen out to dinner after we visit Grandpa? As a thank you for bringing the piano?"

"We'd love to go out to eat after, but call me old-fashioned—I'd feel weird about you paying for me. How about you treat Owen, and I'll pay for you and me?"

Maggie smiled. "Deal."

Maggie couldn't wait for Joel and Owen to get to her office on Tuesday. For one reason, she was excited to see Joel, but she was also looking forward to Hadley meeting him.

At almost four o'clock, Maggie's phone rang.

"Hey!" Maggie answered.

"We're here—out in the parking lot."

"I'll be right out."

"K—bye."

Maggie ran to Hadley's office.

"They're here!" Maggie exclaimed.

Hadley went outside with her. As they walked toward Joel's truck, he stepped out of the driver's side and left the door open.

"Joel," Maggie said as they got closer, "this is my friend, Hadley."

Joel stuck out his hand and shook Hadley's. "Nice to meet you," he said.

"It's nice to meet you too. I've heard so many things about you—all good!" Hadley said.

Joel smiled. He stepped back and motioned inside the truck. "Hadley, this is my brother, Owen."

Hadley leaned to look in. "Hi, Owen!"

"Hi," Owen said without looking.

Maggie took her key out of her pocket and handed it to Joel.

"Here's my key, and I've already texted you my address. So I guess you're good to go."

"And you just want us to set it in the family room, right?"

"Yeah, I cleared a space for it on one wall. Thank you for

doing this." She leaned past Joel and spoke to Owen. "Thank you so much for helping, Owen."

"You're welcome," Owen said as he stared out the window.

"We'll get going then, and we'll be back by five." Joel kissed Maggie on the cheek. "Good to meet you, Hadley," he added as he got back into his truck.

"You too!" Hadley said.

As the truck drove away, Maggie and Hadley headed back to the office.

"Maggie, he's gorgeous. He's rugged, he's manly, and he loves his little brother." Hadley sighed. "I think I hate you."

Maggie laughed.

At five o'clock, Maggie walked out into the parking lot and found Joel and Owen parked next to her car. Joel got out of the truck.

"Everything go okay?" she asked.

"Went great," he said, reaching into his pocket. "Here's your key back, and we already returned Sage's after we'd loaded the piano."

Maggie took the key and put it back on her keyring. "I can't thank you two enough for handling all of that for me."

Joel smiled. "We're happy to help."

"Would you and Owen want to ride with me so you don't have to pull the trailer over to Grandpa's? Then I can bring you back here to get your truck after we eat."

"That sounds good." Joel leaned into the truck. "Hey, Owen, we're gonna ride with Maggie now to visit her grandpa."

Owen didn't move.

"Then after that," Joel continued, "could you help us pick out a place to eat dinner?"

Owen opened his door. "Mom always said I was a great helper."

"You definitely are," Joel agreed.

The three of them loaded into Maggie's car and headed to the memory care facility.

"We're here to visit Liam Shaw," Maggie told the receptionist as she signed their names on the visitor sheet.

The lady at the desk smiled and nodded as she wrote Maggie's name on a sticker and handed it to her. Then she looked at the visitor sheet and wrote two more name tags for Joel and Owen. Joel helped Owen put his sticker on his shirt.

Maggie led the way to her grandpa's room. His door was closed, so she knocked lightly. Just as she was about to push the door open, Patricia opened it.

"I was thinkin' it was about time for you to get here, Ms. Maggie. And you've brought some friends with you!" Patricia said, smiling at Joel and Owen.

Maggie looked past Patricia and saw her grandpa sitting in his chair. He was still in his pajamas, and his hair hadn't been brushed. He was leaning forward and looked upset.

"Yes, umm . . . Patricia, this is my boyfriend, Joel, and my good friend, Owen," said Maggie.

Joel smiled as Owen stared down to the side.

"Oh, I am so, so glad to meet you both," Patricia said.

"It's nice to meet you, too," Joel replied.

"How is he today?" Maggie asked. "I was wanting Grandpa

to meet Joel, but maybe this isn't a good time."

"Well, he's havin' a hard day again. He won't let me help him change clothes or comb his hair, and he . . ."

As Patricia spoke to Maggie and Joel, Owen walked unnoticed into Liam's room and sat down in a chair facing Maggie's grandpa.

"Hi," Owen said, staring right at Liam's face.

Liam didn't respond. He was bent forward and wringing his hands.

Joel realized Owen was no longer standing beside him in the hallway. He looked into the room and saw Owen sitting with Maggie's grandpa.

Patricia was telling Maggie and Joel, "He hasn't been able to speak today. I tried to—" when Joel raised his hand and said, "I'm so sorry to interrupt. Excuse me—" He leaned into the room. "Owen? Owen, let's come back out here into the hall."

Owen ignored him.

"Are you going to die soon?" Owen asked Liam in his straightforward tone.

"Owen—" Joel stepped into the room, but Maggie placed her hand on his arm to stop him.

"Joel," Maggie said softly. "Look at Owen."

Owen wasn't looking down to the side like he usually did. He was staring directly into Liam's face.

Maggie's grandpa raised his head a little.

"Yes," Liam answered weakly.

"Are you scared to die?" Owen asked in his unmoving voice.

Liam lifted his head all the way until he was sitting upright. He looked at Owen. Liam's eyes brightened, and his expression relaxed.

"No," said Maggie's grandpa. "I'm not scared at all. I know where I'm going, and I'll get to see my Jane again."

Maggie gasped as she covered her mouth.

"I'll get to see my son, Jacob, and my daughter-in-law, Rebekah," Liam continued, his voice still weak. "No, I'm not scared. I'm looking forward to going to Heaven."

"My mom is in Heaven too." As Owen spoke, he kept his eyes glued on Liam's face. "I miss her." Owen swallowed hard. "I want to go to Heaven now so I can be with her."

Joel drew a sharp breath as Maggie clung tightly to his arm. Tears ran down her face. She looked at Joel and noticed his eyes were red and glistening.

Liam's expression softened even more. "Oh, no, no, young man. It's not your time yet. Your mom wouldn't want you to come see her yet. She wants you to live a long, happy life and be a great helper to others."

Joel and Maggie glanced at each other in astonishment.

"Mom always said I was a great helper," Owen said, still staring at Liam.

"I bet you are, and that's what would make your mom very proud—to watch her son down here, helping others." Liam placed his hands on his lap, sitting fully upright—like he used to. His voice sounded more energized. "If you're a believer in Christ, you'll see your mom again, but you've got to wait until God says it's time. Okay?"

"Okay," said Owen.

"I feel God telling me that *my* time is coming soon," Liam said.

"Will you tell my mom I said hello, and I love her?" Owen asked, his eyes still fixed on Liam's face.

Liam smiled. "I sure will, son. I sure will."

Maggie sniffed loudly, causing Liam to glance over at the doorway where she, Joel, and Patricia were standing, their faces and shirts covered with tears.

"Oh! Maggie-Girl!" said Liam, his eyes still bright. Noticing her crying, his expression changed. "What's wrong, Magnolia Jane?"

"Nothing." Maggie wiped her face and chuckled. "Absolutely nothing."

She took Joel's hand and guided him into the room. Owen stood, looking down to his side.

"Grandpa, I'd like you to meet my boyfriend, Joel Barrett, and this is his brother, Owen."

Liam slowly reached his hand out to Joel.

"It's nice to meet you," he said, shaking Joel's hand.

Chapter 25

Maggie and Joel sat side by side in the booth of the fast-food place Owen had picked. They quietly watched as Owen, sitting across from them, happily ate his chicken nuggets and tater tots. There was so much to say, yet at the same time, both Joel and Maggie were at a loss for words. The moving scene of Owen and Liam had them completely overwhelmed.

"Joel," Owen said as he ate a tater tot.

"Yeah, Owen?"

Owen glanced quickly at Joel's face and then back at his food. "Are you mad?"

"No, not at all."

"You're not talking."

Joel inhaled and exhaled. "I'm just . . . I'm feeling really happy. I'm glad I got to meet Maggie's grandpa, and I'm glad you got to talk to him."

"I'm glad too," Maggie said as she leaned against Joel's arm.

She looked at Owen. "Are you excited about your cousin's wedding, Owen?"

"Yes."

"Now, will this be a dancing reception or a no-dancing reception?" Maggie asked Joel.

"I think there will be slow dancing," Joel answered, grinning. "Will you please dance with me?"

"Yes, I will."

"And will you dance with me too, Maggie?" Owen asked while he chewed a bite of a chicken nugget and stared at his food.

Maggie looked at Owen in surprise and then at Joel.

Joel's shocked expression turned into an amused smile.

"I would love to," Maggie said with a grin.

To her delight, a small smile crossed Owen's face as he ate another tater tot.

The following night, Joel called before Maggie went to sleep.

"I have great news!" said Maggie.

"What's that?"

"I think Grandma's car finally sold!"

"Oh, great!"

"Yeah, a guy called today while I was on my lunch break. He's gonna meet me at the house Saturday afternoon to pay and get the car."

"What time?"

"Two o'clock."

"Want me to come?" Joel asked. "To make sure you're safe?"

Maggie smiled. "Yes, please."

"You got it, babe."

"Thank you."

"No problem. Hey, guess what I've been doing this evening?"

"What?" Maggie asked.

"I've been teaching Owen how to slow dance."

"Have you really? Oh, I love it!"

Joel laughed, then went quiet. After a few seconds, he said, "Maggie, I think his light is back." His voice broke as he spoke. "We, uh . . . we witnessed a miracle yesterday. Didn't we?"

"We did," Maggie said softly.

Maggie wore a fitted, long, dark-green silk dress to Kyle's black-tie wedding. She had her hair pinned to the side and wore an elegant gold bracelet and earrings. The evening ceremony took place inside a Mediterranean-style building.

Joel had been busy with all the pre-wedding photos, so she hadn't seen him that day yet. She did, however, spot Ray, Joel's dad, as she took her seat. He waved at her from his seat near the front.

The ceremony started.

After the grandparents and parents were seated, Owen came down the aisle. He looked handsome in his tux but also tense. He stared down to the side. Two more grooms-men followed. Then, Joel walked down the aisle. He looked incredible in his tux. After he took his place at the front, he saw Maggie. When their eyes met, he smiled in a way that always made her heart skip a beat.

Joel had more wedding photos after the ceremony, so Maggie walked to the next room where the reception was being held. It was a large ballroom with a dance floor on the right and round tables and chairs on the left. She paused at the en-trance to look at a photo display of Kyle and his beautiful new wife, Tiffani. They were such a gorgeous couple.

Leaving the photo display, Maggie found her place card at one of the round tables and took her seat. She glanced at the other cards at her table. The seat next to hers was Joel's, with Owen beside him, and Ray sat next to Owen. On her other side was a woman named Linda Barrett, and next to her was a place for Dave Barrett.

Must be Joel's extended family.

Maggie took a slow breath in and out. She was excited to meet Joel's extended family, but also nervous.

The ballroom quickly filled with guests.

"You must be Maggie!" a woman said as she approached her.

Maggie stood. "Yes, ma'am."

The lady gave Maggie a small hug and said, "I'm Joel's Aunt Linda. And this," she motioned to the man behind her, "is Joel's Uncle Dave."

Dave shook Maggie's hand. "It's nice to meet you, Maggie."

"It's nice to meet you too," Maggie replied.

Linda and Maggie sat down at the table as a man came over to talk to Dave.

"Maggie, let me tell you," Linda said, "you have made our Joel so very happy. He just lights up when he talks about you!"

Maggie smiled. "He makes me very happy too."

Linda was about to say something when the emcee got on his mic and asked everyone to take their seats. It was time to introduce the wedding party.

The groomsmen were announced, followed by the bridesmaids. They formed a line on one side of the dance floor. The bride and groom were then introduced, and as they made their way to the dance floor, the emcee played a slow song. The couple immediately went into their first dance. Throughout the entire dance, Joel kept his eyes locked on Maggie's.

When their dance ended, the emcee announced that dinner would now be served. As the wedding party walked to their seats, Maggie stood up to greet Joel with a hug. He walked toward her, his eyes never leaving hers. She reached out and hugged him, and he whispered in her ear, "You're the most stunning woman I've ever seen in my life."

After the meal and cake cuttings, the emcee announced that the dance floor was open. Joel wiped his mouth with his cloth napkin and turned to Owen.

"Owen, I'm gonna ask Maggie to dance first, okay?"

"Okay. I'll ask her next," Owen said.

Joel nodded. "Perfect."

Maggie smiled as Joel turned to her. He stood and stuck out his hand. "Maggie, my love, will you please do me the honor?"

Aunt Linda put her hands together and said, "Ahh," as Maggie giggled and stood, taking his hand.

On the dance floor, Joel held Maggie close—his one hand around her back, her hand on his shoulder, and her other hand gripping his.

"I love you," he said, gazing into her eyes.

"I love you. You look so handsome."

"Thank you." He leaned down to her ear and whispered, "I'm the proudest man in this room to have *you* in my arms."

Maggie smiled, gave him a quick kiss on his neck, then rested her head against his chest, where it stayed for the remainder of the song.

When the song ended, Joel said, "Maggie, would you mind sitting back down? Owen practiced asking you to dance."

"Sure!"

Maggie weaved her way through the crowd and took her seat. Joel sat beside her and nodded at Owen. Owen stood and stiffly walked over to Maggie.

He glanced at her face and then down to the floor as he said, "Maggie, I would be happy for you to dance with me."

"That would make me very happy too, Owen," Maggie said as she stood up.

She followed him to the nearest edge of the dance floor. He turned and stood still, looking down to the side. Maggie reached out her hand for him to hold and placed her other hand on his shoulder. He gently put one hand on her waist and took her other hand. They slowly started leaning side to side. They stood so far apart that two more people could have easily fit between them, but the moment—the dance—didn't feel awkward at all. It felt . . . precious.

Chapter 26

The night of Kyle and Tiffani's wedding felt like a dream—the entire evening was perfect. Maggie stayed with Sage that night and then went to church with her the following morning.

Maggie was overcome with joy during the sermon when she glanced at who was sitting with her—Sage was on her left with Joyce next to her, and Joel was on her right with Owen and Ray beside him. She felt as if she were sitting in church with family again. She hadn't felt this way in years.

After the service, the six of them went to eat lunch together at Tina's Diner. When the meal was over, Maggie got into her car and began the three-hour drive back to her apartment. Leaving Jasper was getting harder and harder. What used to feel like heading home had started feeling like leaving home.

The week flew by quickly. Maggie visited her grandpa on Tuesday and Saturday. Both visits were difficult. He was having trouble not only speaking but also eating now. Watching dementia take him away, piece by piece, was absolutely awful, but it wasn't the hardest part. His eyes—looking into them was the most difficult. They looked so scared, so lost, so tired.

Since his diagnosis, she'd begged God to please let him stay with her as long as possible, but since hearing his conversation with Owen, Maggie's prayer had shifted to asking God to please take him gently when it was time. Maggie knew that time would be soon.

Maggie didn't go to Jasper after visiting her grandpa on Saturday because Hadley's older sister was having a baby shower that afternoon, and Joel was helping his uncle Dave lay new flooring at his and Linda's house. Maggie and Joel talked on the phone, of course, but this was the first weekend they hadn't seen each other since they'd started dating.

As Maggie was getting out of bed to get ready for work on Monday morning, her phone rang. She immediately feared it was Patricia calling about her grandpa, but it wasn't. It was Joel.

"Hello?"

"Good morning," said Joel.

"Everything okay? You don't usually call me this early."

"Yep, just had you on my mind and wanted to tell you how much I love you before I go to work."

Maggie grinned. "I love you too. Got a big day?" she asked,

putting on her slippers.

"Got a big job. I'm glad Kyle's back from his honeymoon. We'll need him today."

Maggie heard his truck start.

"Well, I won't keep you," he said. "Bye, babe."

"Bye."

A couple of hours later, Maggie was at work, sitting at her desk. She was designing social media posts for a new client. Her phone rang, but she didn't know the number.

"Hello?"

"Maggie?"

She didn't recognize the voice, but whoever it was sounded panicked.

"Yes, this is Maggie."

"Maggie, it's Ray." His voice was strained. "There's been an accident . . . Joel's hurt."

Maggie felt like she'd been hit in the chest with a baseball bat.

"Is he—is he okay?"

"I don't know," Ray answered.

She could hear him choking up.

"Ray, where are you? Where's Joel?"

"Owen and I are following the ambulance. Could you please come to the hospital? Kyle's hurt too. He's in another ambulance. Could you—could you please come and stay with Owen?"

Maggie grabbed her purse and ran out of her office. "I'm on my way!"

Maggie sped down the road, her emergency lights blinking. She called Sage once she was calm enough to talk, but lost it again the second Sage answered.

While driving and listening to Sage pray for Joel, Ray beeped in. Without interrupting Sage's prayer, Maggie clicked over to Ray.

"Ray? What's happening?"

"He's in surgery now. They said there's internal bleeding, and they can't find where it's coming from." He sniffed.

"He's—he's gonna be okay, Ray. He *has* to be." Maggie was on the verge of breaking down into tears again, but she forced herself to hold them in.

"That's right." Ray cleared his throat, also trying to compose himself. "Joel's gonna be okay."

"What happened?"

"We checked the tree before Kyle climbed up. It was fine, Maggie. We didn't see anything wrong." He took a breath. "The tree was about sixty feet high. When Kyle was over halfway up, it cracked." Ray exhaled loudly. "It all happened so fast. I saw Kyle falling . . . and Owen . . . Owen wasn't in the truck yet."

Maggie heard Owen loudly say, "Joel didn't tell me to sit in the truck yet, Dad. He didn't tell me, Dad. He didn't tell—"

"You're right, Owen," Maggie heard Ray say calmly. "It wasn't time for you to sit in the truck. You didn't do anything wrong, Owen."

Maggie waited, holding her breath.

"Maggie?" said Ray.

"I'm here."

"The middle of the tree just disintegrated. The whole top half of it was heading toward Owen, so . . . so Joel ran . . . pushed him out of the way." Ray said the next part louder and slower: "I'm very, very thankful that Owen isn't hurt—only got a few knicks and scratches." Maggie knew that Ray was making sure Owen heard him. He lowered his voice again. "But Joel . . . Maggie, Joel was . . . crushed." Ray barely got the last word out. Maggie could hear him crying.

"God, please no," Maggie prayed softly, tears streaming down her face.

Ray cleared his throat again. "We got the tree off of him, and he was still breathing. But—" He lowered his voice again. "It wasn't good, Maggie."

She didn't know what to say. After a few seconds, she asked, "How is—how is Kyle?"

"Somehow, he didn't break his neck or hit his head. God kept him alive. Last I heard from his wife—she's here at the hospital too—was that one of his ankles and both of his legs and hips are broken in multiple places."

Maggie's heart ached for Kyle and his new wife. What a nightmare to happen right after one of the best weeks of their lives.

"Ray, I'll be there as quick as I can."

"You just be careful driving, okay?"

"Yes, I will."

"We're in the surgical waiting room," Ray added.

"Okay, bye."

Maggie hung up and sobbed.

Once she'd calmed back down a bit, she called Hadley and asked her to pray. Then she called Sage back and updated her. Sage stayed on the phone with Maggie for the rest of the drive. Maggie made the three-hour drive to Jasper in about two and a half hours.

She parked her car and sprinted into the hospital, following the signs to the surgical waiting area. There, she found Ray and Owen sitting in the corner. Ray had blood stains on his shirt and pants. Owen's shirt was dirty and ripped, and his arms were covered in scrapes and dirt.

"How is he?" Maggie asked as she quickly walked over to them.

Ray stood. "They've stopped the bleeding." He wiped his forehead. "They're now working on his arm and his leg."

A nurse came into the waiting room.

"Mr. Barrett?" she asked.

"Yes," Ray answered, walking over to her.

"The doctor needs to speak with you, please."

Ray turned to Maggie. "Will you stay with Owen?"

Before Maggie could answer, Owen stood and, looking to the side, adamantly said, "No. I'm going with you, Dad. I'm going with you. I'm going with you. I'm going with—"

Ray walked over and put his hands on Owen's shoulders. "Listen. Listen, Owen," he said calmly. "I need you to please stay here, okay? I'll be right back. Maggie's gonna stay with you." Ray let go of his shoulders and followed the nurse. "I'll be right back," he called to Owen as he walked out of the waiting room.

"Mmmmmmm, mmmmm . . ." Owen started making an intense humming sound—almost more of a moan. Then he hit his head with his hand.

"Owen!" Maggie exclaimed.

He slapped his head again.

"Owen, please don't do that," she pleaded.

He kept making the forceful humming sound as he turned and banged his forehead against the wall—over and over.

"Owen! Please! Please stop! Please—I—I need your help, Owen!" Maggie shouted to his back.

Owen stopped making the guttural moan and froze in place.

"I need your help, please," Maggie said calmly. "I'm really

worried, and I need you to help me calm down."

He didn't move.

"Can you please help me?"

Owen turned toward her, looking to the side. His forehead was bright red, and tears tracked down his cheeks.

"Mom . . . Mom always said I was a great helper," he said softly.

"Yes. Yes, you are. And I really need your help right now."

He glanced at her eyes and then looked back down.

Maggie had bought two books about autism a few weeks ago and had been studying them. She'd read that some autistic people find firm pressure calming.

"I think, Owen," she swallowed, "that if I could give you a hug, that would make me feel less scared."

Owen didn't say anything or move.

"Could I try it?" she asked calmly.

Owen glanced at her eyes again, then back down.

"Okay," he said softly.

Owen didn't move. He stood with his arms at his sides. Maggie slowly wrapped her arms around him and rested her hands on his back. He was so much broader and taller than her that only her palms touched his back. She turned her head to the side and rested it against his chest. She gently squeezed with her arms, gradually increasing the pressure.

They stood like that for the next ten minutes.

Chapter 27

The doctor spoke with Ray, preparing him for the possibility of having to amputate Joel's left leg. However, after long hours of intense surgery, the surgical team managed to save his leg by inserting multiple rods and pins. They also placed a rod in his left arm.

Making huge, life-changing decisions while under extreme stress is never a good idea, and yet, that's exactly what Maggie did. On the day of Joel's accident, as she'd sat in the hospital's waiting room with Ray, Owen, and Sage—Sage had shown up about an hour after Maggie arrived—Maggie felt the most calming clarity that she'd ever experienced in her life. She knew exactly what she had to do.

Once Joel's surgery was complete and he was stable, he was moved to a room. A nurse came to the waiting area to let them know they could go back and see him for a few minutes if they'd like. It was close to midnight, so Sage gave Maggie a hug, spoke a few words to Ray and Owen, and then headed home.

Maggie, Ray, and Owen followed the nurse to Joel's room as she explained that he was heavily sedated for pain control. He had also been intubated to protect his airway from the accident trauma and pain medications. The left side of his body had taken the brunt of the tree's weight and had basically been crushed. He was covered in bruises and swelling, but aside from a two-inch cut in front of his left ear, his face was unscathed.

After entering the room, Ray motioned for Maggie to go first. She gently kissed Joel's forehead and whispered in his ear, "I love you." She moved over so Ray could speak to him next.

Ray leaned in close to Joel's ear and said, "You're gonna be okay, buddy. You're gonna be okay. You just concentrate on gettin' better." He stood up and looked over at Owen. "You wanna say something to him, Owen? He can't talk back to us right now, but I bet he can hear us."

Ray put his hand on Owen's back and gently guided him next to Joel's bed. Owen slowly bent down to Joel's ear and said, "You did not tell me to get in the truck."

Ray made eye contact with Maggie as they both smiled.

Before Sage had left the hospital, she'd offered for Maggie to stay at her house, but Maggie had declined.

"I need to go check on Grandpa tomorrow, and I have some things I have to take care of. But thank you," Maggie had said.

As she drove home in the wee hours of that Tuesday morning, she mentally worked out all of the details of her plan.

Maggie pulled into her apartment's parking lot around 5:00 a.m. She didn't lie down. Instead, she took a shower and got ready for the day. After putting on her makeup, she packed everything she could think of needing for the week and loaded it into her car.

On her way to work, she stopped for a coffee and a pastry. She had time to go inside, order, and sit down to eat. Once seated, she called Hadley. She wanted to explain her plan to Hadley first before putting it into action. After their conversation, Maggie texted her boss to ask if she could come speak with her that morning.

Maggie knocked on Mrs. Anderson's office door.

"Come in," she heard.

"Ahh, Maggie," her boss said after Maggie opened the door. "Come on in and have a seat."

Maggie closed the door and sat in the closest of the two chairs facing Mrs. Anderson's desk.

"Thank you for meeting with me," Maggie said. "And thank you for letting me leave so quickly yesterday."

Mrs. Anderson nodded. "How's your boyfriend doing?"

Maggie glanced to the side as she took a breath. "Not good." She swallowed.

"You've had a hard couple of months, Maggie."

"Yes, ma'am. And you've been so understanding. Thank you." Maggie shifted in her seat. "I wanted to talk with you and see if there's any way I could start working remotely."

Maggie tried reading Mrs. Anderson's face, but her expression didn't change.

"I need to move to Jasper," she continued. "Joel's going to need a lot of help while he's recovering, and that's going to take a while. And his dad will need help caring for him and his younger brother." Maggie paused, but Mrs. Anderson said nothing. "I love my job here, but . . . I know my future is in Jasper. If there's any way that I could possibly have both—well, I just had to ask."

Mrs. Anderson leaned back in her seat as she watched Maggie. "Is he the one?"

Maggie smiled. "Yes, ma'am. He is."

Mrs. Anderson nodded. "Maggie, you've worked here for . . . how many years now?"

"Four years."

"Four years," Mrs. Anderson repeated. "And you've done a wonderful job. You always finish your work on time, and you're easy to work with." She leaned forward again. "I'm going to take some time and think this through. I'll let you know my decision this afternoon."

"Thank you," Maggie said, standing.

Maggie left her boss's office, closed the door, and turned to walk down the hall. She was immediately face-to-face with a sobbing Hadley, who threw her arms around Maggie.

"I want you to be happy, and I understand why you have to go," Hadley said between sniffs. "But I *hate* this."

"I know," Maggie said as she patted Hadley's back. "I can't imagine not seeing you almost every day." She stepped back to look at her friend. "But I'll come back here lots to see you and visit Grandpa."

"Promise?" Hadley asked, black mascara flowing down her cheeks.

"I promise. And you'll come visit me in Jasper too, right?"

"Of course!" Hadley said as she wiped her face with a

balled-up tissue. "Maybe I'll find my man in Jasper too."

They laughed and hugged again.

Hadley went into the restroom to clean her face, while Maggie headed to her office and called Ray.

"How is he this morning?" she asked.

"'Bout the same. The nurse said he won't be havin' conversations with us for a few days because they're keepin' him sedated to help him with the pain."

"How's Owen?"

"My brother, Dave, came and picked him up last night, so he's at their house." Ray sounded exhausted.

"Have you been able to get any rest?" Maggie asked.

"I've dozed off and on some in this chair here."

"Well, when I get off work, I need to swing by and check on my grandpa, and then I'll head your way. I can stay with Joel tonight so you can go home and rest."

She heard Ray breathe out.

"Are you sure, Maggie? I know you work and live a ways from here."

"I'm sure," she answered. "I want to be there."

Chapter 28

About an hour before the workday ended, Mrs. Anderson called and asked Maggie to come to her office.

"Have a seat," she said as Maggie closed the door. "I've given your situation some thought, and I've made a decision."

Maggie held her breath.

"Your annual review is next month," Maggie's boss continued. "I'd already decided that you'd receive a raise at your review, but instead, I'm going to allow you to work remotely. I feel that's a fair swap because not having to come into the office is a perk. But I'd like for us to try this new arrangement for a three-month trial period. I've never had an employee work long-term or permanently from home, but I'm willing to give this a try. How's all of that sound to you?"

"It sounds great," Maggie said, her voice filled with a mix of gratitude and relief. "Thank you."

The next morning, Maggie left the hospital after spending the night there to embark on a day of phone calls. First, Maggie contacted her real estate agent, Tony, and let him know that she wouldn't be selling her grandmother's house after all.

"I've decided to move into the house," Maggie told him.

"I think that's a fine idea, and we both know the lady in the house next door to you will be thrilled." Tony chuckled.

The next call Maggie made was to Sage, who squealed when she heard the news. At the end of their conversation, Sage said, "Well, goodbye, neighbor!" and squealed again.

Then Maggie called to have Wi-Fi set up at the house so she could work from home. After that, she called to line up a moving company to bring everything she owned from her apartment to her house.

A week later, Maggie moved into her house. She had the movers put the piano back where it had originally been. When the moving company finished unloading everything and left, the first item Maggie unpacked was the Magnolia bowl Joel had given her. She set it in the middle of her kitchen table.

Since the two upstairs rooms were the same size, she converted her mother's old room into her bedroom. She placed her favorite picture of her parents on her nightstand, and beside that frame, she set a photo of her and Joel from Kyle's wedding.

She put her treadmill, desk, and bookshelves in her grandmother's old bedroom. After unpacking all of her books and arranging them on her shelves, she hung her mom's calligraphy piece on the wall next to her desk. She'd framed the photo that Sage and Joyce had given her—the one of the day her parents met—and hung it next to her mom's artwork.

Maggie unpacked all her dishes and put them into the honey-stained cabinets. With the money she'd made from the estate sale and selling her grandmother's car, she'd have enough to update the kitchen and add a dishwasher.

Before calling it a day, Maggie unboxed four picture frames and spread them out on top of the piano. One was a photo of her and Sage—Joel had taken it for Maggie after church on the Sunday after Kyle's wedding. The second frame showed a photo of Grandpa Liam and Grandma Jane. The next picture was of Owen, Joel, and Maggie taken at the wedding, and the last one was of Hadley and Maggie.

Maggie stepped back and looked at the photos.

"I'm home," she said softly.

Joel's recovery was slow—as expected. A week after his surgery, the doctor had the nurses lessen his pain medications, so Joel was finally "there" and able to really talk with Ray, Owen, and Maggie. Since the accident, they'd come by daily at different times to check on him. On weekdays, Maggie would go to the hospital in the morning before starting her workday and stay for about an hour. Then she'd return every evening to eat dinner with Joel.

On Saturday mornings, Maggie went to visit her grandpa and would stay with him for a couple of hours. Then she'd meet Hadley to eat lunch before driving back to Jasper.

At her first morning visit, when Joel was conscious, he said groggily, "I'm so glad you're here, but please don't get fired because of me."

Maggie smiled. "Oh, that reminds me," she said as she straightened his bedding before gently sitting next to him—on his good side. "I found the perfect person to move into my grandmother's house."

"You did? It sold?"

Maggie nodded. "Sort of. There's now a twenty-six-year-old woman living there. She's a graphic designer who works remotely, and she has this beautiful Magnolia bowl sitting on her kitchen table."

She saw the muscles tighten in Joel's throat and jaw as he tried to compose himself. A tear rolled down his cheek.

"I love you," he whispered.

Maggie gently and carefully kissed him.

Ray and Owen stopped by to visit Joel for an hour or two each day. On weekdays, it was either during their lunch break or after work.

On one of their lunch visits, Ray wanted to talk about the business.

"I've been thinking," Ray said as he sat in a chair next to Joel's hospital bed, holding his half-eaten sub sandwich.

"The doctor said your recovery is going to take a long time, and even when you're as healed as you can be—" He paused, trying to figure out how to word things. "You may not be physically able to work like you used to."

Joel nodded, looking down at his bed. He held his sandwich in his right hand, but hadn't eaten much of it. Thankfully, Joel was right-handed, so his accident at least hadn't taken the use of his dominant hand.

"So, I was thinking, *you* should be our new paperwork, office hire. Makes sense—doesn't it? We need someone to take over the job your mom used to do, and without havin' to be out in the field now, you'd be able to do it. Then, after some time, if you wanted to try your old job again, you could. And we could hire someone else to do the bookkeepin'."

"What are *you* gonna do, though, Dad? With Kyle and me out, you're shorthanded."

"Uncle Dave's been helpin' us out, and so has Parker."

Parker was Uncle Dave's youngest son. He'd recently graduated from high school and was still figuring out what he wanted to do.

"Parker's a quick learn," Ray added before taking a bite of his sandwich.

Joel thought for a bit. "I'm not an office guy, or at least I didn't used to be. But this sounds like a good plan—if you're sure this'll work out well for you."

"It'll be just fine." Ray looked Joel in his eyes. "*You're* gonna be just fine." He grinned. "You gotta be, and you gotta have a job 'cause you got a sweet lady who sure does seem to love you."

Joel smiled. "I do. And I love her."

Ray nodded. "Ya found a keeper, Joel."

Ray wadded up the wrapper of his sandwich and tossed it in the garbage. He picked up his soda bottle to get another drink, but it was empty.

"Gonna go get me another drink from the machine. You

two need anything?" he asked, glancing at Owen and then Joel.

"No," said Owen, mid-chew of his chicken nugget.

"I'm good," Joel said.

Ray left the room, leaving the brothers alone.

"Owen," said Joel.

Owen didn't look at him, but Joel knew he was listening.

"What do you think of Maggie?"

Owen swallowed his food. "She loves you. She looks at you like Mom looked at Dad." He took another bite.

Joel smiled at Owen's insight, stated in his typical matter-of-fact tone.

"Do you like her?" Joel asked.

"Yes." Owen picked up his drink. "And she likes me too."

Joel nodded. "Yes. Yes, she does."

One Sunday, after Maggie and Joel had finished watching his church's service on Maggie's laptop, Joel was unusually quiet.

"Something on your mind?" she asked after a few moments of silence.

"You think I'll ever be able to play the guitar again?"

Maggie thought. His hand was the only part of his left side that didn't have any broken bones, but his left arm had taken a lot of damage. "Have you asked your physical therapist or your doctor about that yet?"

"I did."

"What'd they say?"

"My doctor said she never tells anyone that they 100

percent can or can't do anything, and Logan—my therapist—said there's no way to know until I'm able to try it."

"I think there's a good chance you'll be able to, and you're such a hard worker. If anyone can make it happen, it's you."

Joel gave her a weak smile. His eyes looked defeated. "I'm really trying to keep a positive attitude, but I—I guess I'm feeling down today."

Maggie walked around to the right side of his bed and sat beside him.

"It's okay to feel down and have down days. You've been through a lot." She held his right hand in hers. "And I'm so impressed with how you're handling it all. You've been amazing."

Joel picked up her hand, brought it to his face, and kissed it.

Three weeks after the accident, Kyle was released from the hospital and went home to his new wife. Two weeks later, Joel was discharged as well. Maggie and Owen prepped the house for his return while Ray and Uncle Dave picked up Joel from the hospital.

Since Joel's bedroom was upstairs, Maggie and Owen made the couch in the family room into a bed for him. Then, they moved all of his toiletries from his bathroom upstairs to the guest bathroom next to the family room.

"All righty, I think we're ready for him," Maggie said as she set Joel's hairbrush in the bathroom vanity drawer. "I'm gonna start cooking some dinner for all of us now."

"What are we having?" Owen asked, staring down at his side.

"I'm making ham chowder and cornbread *and* chicken nuggets and tater tots. That sound good?"

"I'll eat the chicken nuggets and tater tots."

"Perfect," said Maggie. "Hey, thanks for letting me help you get the house ready for Joel."

Owen glanced at Maggie's eyes, then down at the ground. "You're a great helper."

Maggie smiled. "Thank you. Want to help me cook?"

"Yes."

Chapter 29

Maggie and Owen had just finished cooking dinner when they heard the garage door open.

"They're home," Owen said as he walked to the kitchen's back door and opened it.

Maggie overheard Ray say, "Hey, Owen, can you come get Joel's bag out of the back of the car?"

Without speaking, Owen went into the garage as Maggie stood next to the kitchen table. She noticed the rug in front of the door and, not wanting Joel to possibly slip on it, hurried over to move it.

Bending down to pick up the rug, she heard Joel's voice say, "Something sure does smell good."

"Maggie and I cooked dinner," said Owen.

"Did ya now?" Ray asked.

"Yes."

Maggie set the rug in the laundry room next to the

kitchen. When she returned to the kitchen, she saw Ray and Dave helping Joel up the two stairs from the garage.

Joel's face lit up when he saw her, and Ray noticed the change in his expression.

"Now, Dave, how come he doesn't look like that when he sees you or me?" Ray joked.

"Well, have you seen you and me?" Dave replied, his arm holding onto Joel's right arm. "We're not near as pretty as Maggie here is." Dave looked over at Maggie and playfully winked.

"I would have to agree," Joel said as he finally got both of his feet into the kitchen.

"Wanna take a seat here to rest a minute, or wanna try to make it to the couch?" Ray asked.

Joel's face was flushed, and he was breathing hard. "Let's go on to the couch. I can do it."

Once Joel was lying down and settled onto the couch, Ray, Dave, and Owen got their food and sat at the kitchen table to eat. Maggie fixed her and Joel's bowls and set them, along with napkins, two pieces of cornbread, and their drinks, on a tray.

"Here we go," Maggie said as she walked into the family room with the tray in her hands.

"You're welcome to sit in the kitchen at the table with them if you'd like to," said Joel.

"Are you kidding me? They're great company, of course, but I want to be with you."

Joel grinned as Maggie sat down in the chair next to him. She scooted a small table closer and placed his drink and food on it. He reached out his right hand to her. She placed her hand in his, and he closed his eyes.

"Dear Lord," he said. "Thank You for letting me come home. Thank You for Maggie and for this fine meal she and Owen prepared for us. We love You, Lord. Amen."

Maggie opened her eyes and smiled at him. "I'm so glad you're home."

"You and me both," Joel said as he picked up his spoon. "I'm thankful for that hospital, of course, but I hope I never have to stay there again."

After dinner, Dave came into the family room.

"Well, I best be gettin' on," Dave said. "Soup and corn-bread were great, Maggie."

"Thank you. I'm glad you liked them."

"I'm gonna stop by and check on Kyle on my way home," Dave said.

"Hey . . ." Joel stuck out his right hand. "Thanks for helping me get home, Uncle Dave."

"You betcha," Dave said as he shook Joel's hand.

"Please tell Linda I said hello," said Maggie.

"And tell Kyle I'll see him tomorrow at physical therapy," Joel added. "I think we'll be there at the same time."

"Will do," Dave said as he headed back to the kitchen to tell Ray and Owen goodbye.

Maggie gathered their dishes and arranged them on the tray.

"I'll be back in a bit. I'm gonna clean up the kitchen," she said, standing and picking up the tray.

"Dad won't let you. His rule has always been that

whoever cooks doesn't clean up."

"Well, I'll at least try to help," she said, heading toward the kitchen with the tray of dishes.

Joel was right. Maggie set the tray down on the counter, began tidying up the kitchen, and was immediately and sweetly sent back to the family room to rest.

"Told you," Joel said with a teasing smile as Maggie and Owen both sat down in chairs near the couch.

"Owen, you know what I've been missing?" said Joel.

Owen didn't look at him or answer, but he did turn his head more toward Joel.

"I've been missing watching that Lego building competition with you." Joel glanced at Maggie. "Would you watch it with us?"

"I'd love to!"

Owen flapped his hands as he stood up to get the remote. Maggie had learned that Owen only did that motion when he was happy and excited.

After about ten minutes of watching an episode, Ray came in and sat down.

"What'd I miss?" he asked. "Our favorite team still in it?"

Maggie smiled at him.

Oh my word, I love this family!

"Yeah, I think they might be eliminated in this challenge, though," Joel answered.

"It's going to fall," Owen said as he rocked back and forth, watching the TV.

"Well, their foundation's unstable. Just look at it!" Ray exclaimed.

After two more episodes, Ray stood and stretched.

"I got some stuff I gotta do outside," he said. "Won't take me long. Let me know who gets cut when I come back in."

As he went out the kitchen door, Joel looked at Maggie. "Can I ask a favor?"

"Of course," Maggie answered.

"Could you make me some popcorn?"

"I'm on it!" Maggie said as she stood. "Owen, would you like some too?"

"Yes."

"Coming right up!" said Maggie, heading to the kitchen.

"Thanks!" Joel called. "It's in the pantry!"

After Maggie left the family room, Joel whispered, "Owen, can you quietly come here and kneel down? I need to talk to you."

Owen paused the TV, walked over to the couch, and knelt down beside Joel, staring at the ground.

"I have something important I need to do," Joel whispered. "But I can't do it without your help. Could you sneak up to my room and get a small navy-blue box from my bottom nightstand drawer? And quietly bring it down here to me? I don't want Maggie to see it at all, okay?"

"Okay."

Owen stood and went upstairs.

Chapter 30

Owen came down the stairs with the box hidden behind his back. He quietly walked over to Joel, bent down, and handed him the box, which Joel took and quickly hid under the cushion beside him.

"Thanks, Owen," Joel whispered. "Listen, I need to ask Maggie a very important question, and I'd like for her and me to be alone when I ask her."

"You're going to ask her to marry you," Owen whispered, staring at the couch.

Joel smiled. "That's right. Do you think she'll say yes?"

"Yes."

"Would you mind waiting upstairs in your room while I ask her?"

Owen glanced at Joel's face, then down at the couch. "I don't mind." He stood up and walked back to the stairs.

Joel ran the fingers of his right hand through his hair and then straightened his shirt. His heart was pounding in his chest. This wasn't at all how he'd originally planned to ask Maggie, but for weeks, he'd been telling himself that the day he left the hospital and was able to get back home, that would be the day he would ask her. That thought honestly kept him going. It made Joel not want to give up or surrender to the sadness of his situation. The accident had proven to him how short life is, and he wasn't going to wait one more day to ask her to be his wife.

A few minutes later, Maggie came back from the kitchen, carrying three bowls of popcorn.

"Oh, where'd Owen go?" she asked, glancing around the room.

"He needed something upstairs. He'll be right back."

Maggie placed Owen's bowl next to his chair, handed Joel's to him, and sat back down as she ate a handful of popcorn from her bowl.

Joel "accidentally" dropped his bowl, spilling popcorn on the floor.

"Oh, good grief! Maggie, I'm so sorry."

"That's okay!" she said, hopping up. "I'll make more."

Maggie set her bowl on the coffee table and knelt in front of Joel. She picked up his bowl from the floor and scooped popcorn into it.

"There's some popcorn here on the couch, too, that I can't reach," said Joel.

Maggie sat back on her heel, looked up, and was startled by the sight of Joel holding an open ring box out to her.

"I know I should be the one down on *my* knee," Joel said slowly, "but I don't think I'll be able to do that for a while. And I can't wait until then to ask you."

Maggie's hand covered her mouth.

Joel looked at the box in his hand. "I bought this ring a couple of weeks after you told me you loved me." His eyes returned to hers. "I knew." He swallowed. "I knew you were the only one for me. I didn't want to steal any of Kyle and Tiffani's thunder, so I planned on asking you the weekend after their wedding. And I had this romantic plan, but then"—he motioned to his left side—"this happened. So, I know me sprawled out on the couch in my family room isn't the most romantic of settings, but I can't wait another minute"—his voice broke—"to ask you to be mine. Magnolia Jane Shaw, will you marry me?" A tear escaped his eye as he whispered. "Please? Be my wife?"

Maggie couldn't speak, so she nodded. Tears streamed down her face as she leaned forward and kissed him.

Joel dropped the ring box onto his lap and, with his right hand, wiped her cheeks as she smiled.

"Yes. Yes, I will," Maggie said wholeheartedly.

Joel took the ring out of the box. It was an emerald-cut diamond on a white gold band. He carefully slid the ring onto her shaking finger. It was a little loose.

"We'll get it resized," Joel assured her. "I didn't know how to guess your size without giving you a clue as to what I was doing. I wanted it to be a surprise."

"It was," Maggie said, her smile bigger than it had ever been before in her life. "The perfect surprise. And it is per-fect!" she said, gazing down at the ring on her finger. She looked up at him. "I love you."

"I love you."

"How did you . . . how did you get the ring here on the couch?" Maggie asked. "Was it hidden here the whole time?"

"No, Owen helped me while you were making the popcorn."

"I'm a great helper!" Owen yelled down the stairs, making Joel and Maggie both laugh.

"Yes, you are!" Joel called back. He tucked Maggie's hair behind her ear and caressed her face. "You sure you're ready to join this crazy family?"

"Absolutely."

Epilogue

Joel's body continued healing, growing stronger every week. Walking unassisted at his and Maggie's wedding was his goal, and it kept him focused.

Two months after leaving the hospital, Joel was able to play his guitar again at church. The only difference was that he played while sitting on a stool instead of standing like he always had before the accident. The following Sunday, the bass player showed up with a stool and also sat while playing, which meant a lot to Joel.

Four months after the accident, Joel was able to walk without assistance. He still had some aches, pains, and stiffness—which he'd probably always deal with to some extent—but his body and mind felt strong. He leaned into his new career. No, being an accountant wasn't what he would have chosen, but he was thankful to have a job that let him work with his family. He did find that working inside the house felt monotonous and brought on too much anxiety. For his first week, he tried working from the kitchen table, but the craving to be outside mixed with nonstop worry about Owen's safety made him feel miserable and unfocused.

Maggie said one sentence that fixed the entire situation: "Just because you have an office job now doesn't mean you have to work *in* an office."

The following week, Joel used his cell as a hotspot for his laptop and met the Barrett Tree Service fellas on site. His office was now his truck. Owen would sit with Joel in the cab and wait until the trees were cut into logs. Then Owen would get out and, under Joel's watchful eyes, load the logs. Kyle eventually returned to the family business, and with that, the Barretts were able to put the trauma of the accident behind them.

A few days before Christmas, Maggie's grandpa passed away. Visiting him weekly helped Maggie handle and accept his passing. She felt sadness on Christmas morning, knowing she had no blood relatives left, but she also felt joy for her grandpa, knowing he was enjoying the day with his wife, son, daughter-in-law, and parents. And even though Joel, Sage, Hadley, Owen, and Ray weren't her family by blood, they were her family by love, and she didn't feel alone. She felt blessed.

On June 30, Joel and Maggie were married in an intimate ceremony at their church. Owen was the best man, Hadley was the maid of honor, and Sage sat in the front row as Maggie's honorary grandmother.

The reception was outdoors at a nearby venue. Maggie and Joel had a remembrance table in the entrance of the tent. On the table were four pictures: a photo of Maggie's grandparents—Liam and Jane—one of her parents, and a picture of Joel's mother. The fourth photo was of Edith. Sage had taken it when they were at the beach. Maggie wanted to include the photo of her grandmother on the table, which brought tears of happiness to Sage's eyes. Although Maggie had never met her grandmother and Edith had hurt Maggie's mother terribly, it was because of Edith and the inheritance she'd left that Maggie was where she was today. And for that, Maggie was grateful.

At the reception, Hadley met Sage's grandson, Dylan.

"I gave him my number," Hadley said as she sat down next to Maggie with her plate of wedding cake.

"Who?" Maggie asked.

"Sage's good-looking grandson."

Maggie raised her eyebrows, staring at Hadley.

"What?" Hadley asked defensively.

"The man-child?"

Hadley smiled. "Maybe he and I can grow up together."

Maggie laughed.

"And maybe one day we'll get married, and then I'll live here in this magical town with you!" Hadley exclaimed.

"Oh, I'd love that!"

"Excuse me, ladies," Joel interjected, standing behind them.

Maggie and Hadley both turned.

"May I have this dance?" Joel asked as he extended his hand to his new wife.

"Yes, you may," she said, taking his hand.

As she slow-danced with Joel, her head leaning against his chest, Maggie closed her eyes. She was absolutely overwhelmed with how good God had been to her. Her life had changed so much in a year. She missed her parents and grandparents, of course, but marveled at how God had used every heartache—both hers and theirs—to bring her to this exact moment of joy.

Magnolia Jane

More Books by Holly Jo Flora

A Devotional to Refresh Your Soul & Renew Your Faith

God is always the same—yesterday, today, and tomorrow. He never changes, but we should! God wants us to grow daily in our faith and mature in our relationships.

Same God, New You will help you focus on how our unchanging God can truly transform your life.

Whether you're navigating change, healing from the past, or seeking purpose, this devotional will walk with you every step of the way.

What you'll find inside:

- Daily devotions rooted in Scripture
- Real-life reflections and encouragement
- A fresh start—no matter where you are

Same God, New You
Book Two

Feeling stuck in your spiritual walk?
You are not alone, and you're not forgotten.
Same God, New You – Book Two
is your personal invitation to rediscover
how our unchanging God is still
transforming lives today.

Can a young crow escape a bad reputation,
or will he grow into it?

An unexpected accident forces Jack and his mother
to move to a quiet family farm. Jack is less than thrilled
with their new home. His tendency to ruffle feathers
quickly labels him as a "bad crow."

Jack's mother encourages him to give the farm a
chance, so Jack reluctantly befriends a clever rabbit
named Johnny and a daring squirrel named Alex.
Together, the trio embarks on exciting adventures that
just might help Jack find his place—until one fateful
Christmas Eve when everything spirals out of control.

Now Jack must decide:
Will he embrace his good side or
truly become Jack the Bad Crow?

The Jack the Bad Crow series is an unforgettable
journey full of adventure, laughter, growth, and heart.
This book series is perfect for readers ages 8–12 and fans
of *Charlotte's Web* and *Mrs. Frisby and the Rats of NIMH*.

CLAWTHORNE
A JACK THE BAD CROW STORY

Archie the barn owl has been summoned by the fierce Birds of Prey Council. Their leader, Clawthorne, is an intimidating hawk no one dares to cross. The council's verdict forces Archie to go on an adventure and find help in an unexpected place. Will Archie be able to save his farm family, or will Clawthorne's terrible plan succeed?

Full of heart, hope, and unforgettable characters, this story is perfect for fans of classic tales and epic adventures. Grab your copy of Clawthorne today, and let your imagination soar!

Cystic Fibrosis Activity Book for Kids is a perfect gift for not only children with cystic fibrosis but also for their siblings, cousins, and friends! This high-quality activity book is filled with inspirational, encouraging, and fun sheets—all focused on cystic fibrosis issues. Kids will enjoy spot-the-difference pictures, mazes, coloring sheets, word searches, and much more!

Cystic Fibrosis Activity Book for Kids was created by Holly Jo Flora. Holly Jo's number one goal was to make a cystic fibrosis themed activity book her daughter and son (both have CF) would enjoy. That goal was achieved, and Holly Jo's children have given *Cystic Fibrosis Activity Book for Kids* their stamp of approval. We think your kids will enjoy it too!

Author Holly Jo Flora

Holly Jo Flora loves writing Christian romance, women's devotions, and children's fiction. She lives in Alabama with her husband and their two children.

Subscribe to Holly Jo's newsletter at
hollyjoflora.com

@HollyJoFlora

Acknowledgments

Thank you to my amazing beta readers!
Your feedback was instrumental in
shaping *Magnolia Jane*.

Alex Flora
Madelyn Flora
Derek Flora
Alana Allen
Amanda Allen
Gary Allen
Patricia Allen
Taylor Haynie
Heather Matheny
Cecelia Flora
Beth Flora
Julie May
Robin McAlpin
Laurel Berry
Kylie Jones Hawes
Allison Wilks
Megg Crane
Kayla Wilborn
Anna Hopper
Kendall Hill
Cammie Wilks

Special Thanks to:
Julie May at Anything Creative
Blissfully Serene Spa
The Leesburg Country Store

www.ingramcontent.com/pod-product-compliance
Lightning Source LLC
Chambersburg PA
CBHW021531150726
47990CB00006B/2196